Great
Escapes

Good Housekeeping

Great Escapes

A Short Story Collection

COLLINS & BROWN

First published in Great Britain in 2008
by Collins & Brown
10 Southcombe Street
London W14 0RA

An imprint of Anova Books Company Ltd

The Good Housekeeping website is
www.goodhousekeeping.co.uk

1 2 3 4 5 6 7 8 9

ISBN 978-1-84340-483-5

A catalogue record for this book is available from the British Library.

Typeset by SX Composing DTP, Rayleigh, Essex
Printed by WS Bookwell, Finland

Great Escapes was conceived by Louise Chunn, Emma Dally and Polly Powell

This book can be ordered direct from the publisher. Contact the marketing department,
but try your bookshop first.

www.anovabooks.com

Contents

Man in the Water

Rose Tremain

Rose Tremain is an internationally acclaimed writer. She was educated at the Sorbonne and the University of East Anglia, where she taught creative writing from 1988-95. She has written numerous novels, short-story collections and radio and television plays, and has won many awards for her work. Rose Tremain lives in Norfolk and was awarded a CBE in 2007. Her latest novel is *The Road Home*, now in paperback.

Fishing was my livelihood and my life.

I'd go out early, on the ebb tide. Put up the ragged sail. Hear my boat, the *Mary Jane*, complaining in the wind. Use my telescope to search the sky for gulls. Watch what the other boats were doing. Then, when I had a sniff of how the herring were moving, heave out my nets, heavy and damp, and lower the sail and take up the oars and set the boat's course and wait and listen with my hand on the tiller and watch the corks idling on the water and feel the vastness of the sky all about me.

Now and then, I'd look back at the land: the long girdle of the beach and the Whetstone Lighthouse. Even from far out, I could see the lane where my cottage stood and it would always return to my mind then, that my home was empty of my wife, Hannah, and my bed cold. And I'd ask myself, what are you going to do, you poor man, alone as you are, to prepare your children for their lives? And never any answer came to me. And never, day by day and month by month, did I do one thing for them that I hadn't done before the death of Hannah, because no one gave me counsel as to what I should do. My daughter, Jenny, cooked our meals and washed our linen and hung it to dry in the sun and the salt wind. She was a dutiful girl. But my son, Pips, he only paid attention to his school lessons one day in three and he stole plums from our neighbours and threw pebbles at their dogs and cats and most of the time was no use to any man.

When I brought the boat in with my catch, Jenny and Pips would bring our old grey mare, Hazel, down to the beach with panniers strapped to her sides. We'd tip the herring into the panniers and while I cleaned the *Mary Jane* and piled up my nets and made everything fast against the tide, the children would lead the horse to the Sheds, where the fish was weighed and sold and we'd get our money wrapped in a scrap of paper. And then we'd go home to the empty cottage and brew tea and put slices of bacon to fry, and I'd wash the sea off my hands and out of my eyes and Pips would run around the table, strewing it with knives and forks and cups and saucers, like an elf strewing a dell with leaves, and Jenny would come after him, straightening everything up. I told them they were good children.

On a summer's morning, when I bring the boat in and we've loaded the horse with the catch and Pips is digging for cockles in the sand, Jenny picks up my brass telescope and puts it to her eye and hunts over the ocean with it. I note the stillness of her back, which, at the age of fifteen, is almost the back of a woman, and I look at her sweet head moving left to right, right to left. And then Pips, he stops digging for cockles and says, 'What can you see, Jen?' But she doesn't answer him and I say, 'come on you children, you're not Admiral Nelson. Take Hazel to the Sheds now, and get the catch weighed and paid, then hurry on home.'

And then Jenny, she says quietly, 'Pa, I can see a boat going down and there's a man in the water and I think he's drowning.'

I snatch the telescope from her hands and put it to my eye and Pips, he's jumping up like a puppy dog and saying, 'Give me the spyglass, Pa, for I'd like to see that: a boat going down and a man in the water!' I cuff his head and say, 'What manner of heartless talk is that?'

In the eye of glass I spy something on the distant swell, where Jenny's pointing and it looks like driftwood, but she says, 'No, Pa, no that's a bit of the boat, the bow or the keel of it, sticking up above the waves, and you must get back in the *Mary Jane* and hurry now, or the man in the water will be lost.'

'I see no man in the water,' I say.

'He was there,' she says. 'I saw his head above the waves. I could see his mouth, wide open and crying out.'

So we heave the boat down to the water and Pips jumps in and says, 'I'm coming to help you, Pa,' and I notice his cheeks all scarlet with excitement. But Jenny, she stays where she is on the beach with the horse and begins leading her away up to the Sheds as I get the sail up and turn across the wind.

I give Pips the telescope and show him where I saw what I thought was driftwood and we go fast in the offshore breeze, bumping on the wavelets, and he says: 'This is a rotten instrument, Pa. Nothing stays still in it long enough for me to see the drowning man.' I lower the sail and take up the oars and we go round in circles, staring at the water. Then we start to call out to the man, 'Where are you? Where are you?' But no one replies.

'Reckon he be drowned by now,' says Pips.

I say nothing to this, but nudge the tiller with my elbow, keeping the boat turning and feather the oars to try to steady her in the swell. I don't like the feel of the tide, pulling us out to sea, but we keep on.

★ ★ ★

We found no drowning man and when we got back to Whetstone, no news came of anyone lost at sea that summer morning.

So then I began asking myself, did Miss Jenny invent the man in the water? Did she want me and Pips out at sea so she could sure to be on her own, to go where she pleased for that little while? And I longed more than ever to have my wife back at my side so we could wonder about these things together.

From that day, I kept my eye on Jenny. I saw how she carried herself with her eyes downcast and how, when she was ironing sheets or doing the baking, she would sometimes stare out of the window, in a reverie.

I wanted to ask, 'What are you dreaming of? Or who?' And I longed to say to her, 'Don't leave your Pa. For God knows, I haven't an ounce of an idea how to do anything in the world except fish for herring, and Pips and I, we'd be no good without you. We'd be like hobgoblins.'

In the middle of a cold night, something woke me and I lay there in the dark listening, imagining I heard Jenny's footsteps going along the lane.

I lit my lamp and got up and went to the room where the two children slept in their wooden beds. There was Pips tucked in with the toy he loved, an old bald bear, pressed against his cheek. And there was Jenny, too, asleep with her arm flung upwards on the pillow. So I turned to go back to my room, but suddenly, as I was at the door, she said, 'Pa, what's wrong?'

'Nothing's wrong,' I said. 'Nothing at all.'

I went out early in the *Mary Jane*, at that hour before the dawn has truly come and when I saw the flash of the Whetstone Lighthouse it was then I remembered what Josiah Green, the Keeper of the light, had said to me long ago. Jenny had been eight or nine at that time and pretty as a princess and Josiah had said to me, 'I'll have your daughter for a bride when she's grown, and we'll sail to the West Indies, where I'll make my fortune. And Jenny will have a garden of red lilies and pour tea from a silver tea pot.'

I'd said to Josiah, 'You'll be too old, boy, for a girl of mine.'

And he'd said, 'No man with a fortune is ever too old.'

I sat in my boat and stared up at the lighthouse and imagined Josiah keeping watch over the great burning lights and over the gleaming cogs which rotated the glass. I stared until the sun came up.

* * *

I say to Jenny, 'Teach me how to bake and how to launder. Teach me everything you do.'

'Why, Pa?' she says.

'Just teach me,' I say.

So she ties an apron round me and gets out a mixing bowl and warms it on the range and weighs flour and salt and shows me how to make a well in this for the stirred yeast and fold it slowly in. Then she covers the bowl with a cloth and tells me, 'Now you leave it alone to sponge for a while, then you beat it and knead it, and then you leave it again to rise . . .'

'Sponge and rise? ' I say. 'I don't know what these terms mean . . .'

'No,' Jenny snaps. 'But you will. Or else have no bread.'

When I've kneaded the mix and left it to its rising, Jenny heats up the flat irons and lays a blanket on the table and sets down one of my Sunday shirts and shows me, 'Collar first, then cuffs, then sleeves, then back, then front, then shoulder seams . . .'

'Why is there an order to this?' I ask and she says, 'There's an order to everything. That's what my mother taught me.'

My hands burn and sting, but I try to do what she shows me, to get the shirt smooth, and I see her watching me and then I see the pile of sheets and pillowcases and cloths and petticoats and shawls all waiting to be ironed and I think to myself, how will I do all this drudgery and still keep my livelihood? And I longed to be away from the house, in the *Mary Jane*, alone with my nets and my thoughts.

I turn to Jenny and say, 'Has Josiah Green come courting you?'

She goes to the bread bowl and lifts the cloth and looks to see how far the dough has risen. Then she says, 'Josiah Green is your friend, and a good man.'

'I know,' I say. 'But if he's come courting you, you must tell your Pa.'

'I would tell you,' she says.

I look at her and say, 'Have you always told me the truth, Jenny?'

'Yes,' she says. 'Always.'

I am on to the front of the shirt and I know the front is the most important bit, for it's the only place that can be seen, and how could I go to church on Sunday with my shirt looking like a rag? But my iron's gone cool and won't get the creases out. I stare down at my work, helpless to know what to do, and I hear Jenny sigh and she snatches the iron out of my hand and sets down the second one, scalding hot from the range.

* * *

I went to visit Josiah Green.

I climbed the nine flights of stairs up to the Whetstone Light Room and my footsteps set up an echo that bounced and flew round the building.

I felt my heart and my lungs complaining and nor did I like the chill darkness and containment of the building and once again what I wanted was to be far out on the ocean, with the sky above me.

Josiah was in a cramped little space, where the cogs of the revolving glass were housed, and his head was close to the machinery, listening to it, just like I listened to the birds and the sea. 'Come on, Josiah,' I said, 'I need to talk to you, friend, and I hope you will be honest with me.'

We went up the iron ladder that led to the platform outside the Light Room and the wind came tearing at us and thrilled me. We held to the little railing that kept us from falling to our deaths and I said, 'Are you courting my girl? Yes or no?'

He was silent a while and I let him be. Then he said, 'I love your Jenny and I'd like to leave this lonely job. I'd like to take her with me to the Caribbean Islands and make my fortune before my fiftieth birthday has come and gone.'

I looked down at the waves beating at the foot of the lighthouse and then I said, 'Does my Jenny love you?'

Josiah shielded his eyes against the glare of the sun. 'The truth of it is,' he said, 'I don't know.'

* * *

I go to Jenny in the early evening. New loaves have been baked and all the ironing is freshly done and set in a neat pile.

'Now you must tell your Pa,' I say, 'do you love Josiah Green?'

'No.' she says.

I reach out my hand and stroke her dark hair. 'He could take you to the Indies,' I say, 'and you might be a rich woman and grow scarlet lilies and pour your tea from a silver tea pot.'

'I know,' she says.

'So tell me again then, if this was to be your future, would you love him then?'

'No.' she says.

Her head, under my hand, is warm and beautiful. I take a breath. In that moment of my breath, I hear the familiar sounds of Pips and his friends playing Tag in the lane, as the darkness falls. Then I say to my daughter, 'That morning in summer, when I went chasing after a drowning man, tell me what you saw.'

'I saw a man in the water,' says Jenny.

'Yet there's no body been swept in,' I say, 'and still no report of anyone missing in Whetstone. So tell me the truth, Jenny. Tell me again what you saw.'

She lifts her chin and her dark hair flies as she whips her head away from my caressing hand.

'I saw a man in the water, Pa!' she cries. 'And you can ask me and ask me till the end of time: I saw a man in the water.'

Love Among the Artists

Artists

Fay Weldon

Shakespeare's *Winter's Tale*
brought up to date

Fay Weldon is a novelist, playwright and screenwriter. She worked briefly for the Foreign Office in London, then as a journalist, and then as an advertising copywriter. Fay's work includes over twenty novels, five collections of short stories, several children's books, non-fiction books, magazine articles and a number of plays written for television, radio and the stage, including the pilot episode for the television series *Upstairs Downstairs*. Her latest book, *The Spa Decameron*, is published by Quercus.

A sad tale's best for winter, Shakespeare said, adding that the red blood reigns in the winter's pale, and it was certainly true that year: the Christmas Leo and I broke up for the first time. We were snowed in, there was a power cut that went on for days, and Leo got it into his head that Polix and I were having an affair. Red rage, black heart and cold fingers, while the snowflakes fell and whited everything else except his jealousy, and envy.

You notice I wrote 'for the first time'. It was a tumultuous marriage. You could perhaps compare it to that of D. H. Lawrence and Frieda, who having sought out a cottage in distant Zennor, the better to pursue peace and solitude, then rent the Cornish air with marital discord and terrified visiting friends with the violence of their midnight brawling – only to startle them by being sweet and gay (in the old sense of the word) by breakfast time, no doubt after sex.

Leo and I went to Scotland, not Cornwall, but the

principle was the same. The writer, the artist, needs peace to create. Cut yourself off from the world, from the conveniences and lures of civilisation, build an ivory tower in a world in which ivory is banned, and live in it. Once in it, of course, the artist sets about his own destruction by summoning friends.

Talk about lust, love and revenge amongst the writers! I, by the way, am Hermione, Leo's wife, the one whose unstoppable stage play, *Perdita* – the film just out, the musical on its way, the opera following: merchandising and spin-offs on sale in all appropriate outlets – is currently filling screens and theatres world-wide. I am not as young as I used to be: in fact I got my senior citizen's rail card only this month. I applied for it not because I expected ever to use public transport again – I can snap my fingers and summon the helicopter – but because I feel society owes me something. In fact a great deal. Society gave me a rough time in earlier years: a twelve-year prison sentence on false evidence provided by one's husband is no small thing. I was the victim of a great injustice.

But picture Leo and me back in 1985, before my troubles began, when we were still lovey-dovey – so long as I did exactly as he suggested – baby Max only three months old, holed up in Bohemia Lodge in Midlothian. It was more of a castle than a lodge: all mid-Victorian turrets and battlements, sprites and goblins and no central heating. A benighted age as well as a benighted place.

No mobile phones, no internet, no broadband: just a telephone way out in the servants' quarter of the west wing, an uneasy electricity supply and a postbox a mile away where damp heather met icy swamp. How we lived then! No servants, of course, to fill up the wing: just dusty, frozen rooms, and only me to sweep them.

We hadn't enjoyed our family solitude for more than three weeks when Leo decided he must ask Polix up to Scotland to join us. It made sense. The two men were working in tandem on the script for *Red at Night*. Remember that project? The award- winning TV series on BBC1? It ran for three years, was repeated every Christmas for another five and then the audience lost interest. It fell from view and public favour. These days co-authorship is easy enough – the click of a mouse sends ideas and documents hurtling through space – but then it was a matter of finding envelopes, stamps, and walking a mile to the letterbox. But winter was closing in, and even Leo could see that baby Max came home blue with cold, when I returned from 'doing the post'. I didn't drive, and baby Max couldn't be left behind in case he cried and disturbed the genius at work. Leo liked to work in peace and quiet so peace and quiet was what we most certainly had. But he just hadn't reckoned on snowstorms and power cuts, and no hot water, and the baby crying, and frankly, not much conversation. Women with small babies do not make great conversationalists.

So now there was Leo, Max and Polix for me to look after. Not that Polix was much trouble. He always helped clear up after meals, and drove the five miles to the shops twice a week, so the shopping could be brought back in the car and not wheeled in the pram. He was a gentle, pleasant, thoughtful man, younger than Leo, quite slight and small, with blonde hair tied back in a pigtail. I did not realise at the time the extent of his ambition, his determination to make it in the scripting world. It had always been my own ambition to be a writer. But once we were married Leo said there was only room for one writer in the house and he was obviously the one. He was the genius, I was the muse – and that was the way things were and were going to stay.

The men drank and wrote, and drank and wrote, smoked a certain amount of spliff and I carried logs for the fire and mended fuses, and fed the baby and washed the nappies. Leo didn't approve of domestic machinery, so I did them by hand. Leo really hadn't much good to say about the modern world. And I cooked. I was not born to cook, and it showed. There were still a few leeks in the kitchen garden;

I'd wash them and free them of slugs and grit as best I could but cleaning vegetables in cold water in winter is never fun, and though Polix ate valiantly Leo would make terrible faces. But our lovemaking was the more intense and noisy because of the other male in the house. See what I have, that you haven't!

I had hoped that when *Red at Night* was nearing completion, and talks with the director were to begin, that we could all decamp down south to civilisation, but for some reason Leo decided to bring Camillo to him, not Leo go to Camillo. Camillo was small and smart and all charm, like a mischievous elf, and as gay as all get out.

I realise I haven't told you much about Leo: he looms so large in my mind I can scarcely separate him out from myself. Let me just say he is built on a massive scale, to suit his massive intellect and ego. He is like some great bear wandering through the literary undergrowth, trampling all around. A lesser man than he could be dismissed as an obsessive compulsive, but since he'd won the Booker Prize and a couple of screen-play Oscars, Leo was known as a creative genius, a perfectionist and a national treasure. Let me make it clear: I loved and still love Leo. I'm just one of those tenacious old-fashioned women who weather the storms of marriage for love. Frankly, Leo was just very, very good in bed. Boho Lodge boasted fourteen bedrooms, all vast, all

Fay Weldon

barely furnished, and we had already broken the rusty coiled spring bedsteads in six of them.

Then nothing would do but that Antigonus, who was to play the lead, was asked up as well. He was well built and good looking in a clean-cut kind of way and did his own stunts. More, he was married to my best friend Paulina, which meant she'd come along as well. Sensibly, she never let him out of her sight. And that was good: she was a bold red-haired actress, noisy, talented and kind; at last, another woman, someone to talk to, someone to help cope with Boho Lodge. I walked all the way to the post to send a letter warning them to bring their woollies. But now we were to be six, plus one baby.

There were ancient sheets in ancient cupboards: they needed washing but how could I ever dry them? I aired them and shook them and put them on such beds as were still unbroken. I found mouldy blankets and scraped off the worst of the green. Max developed croup and the doctor was called and suggested a warmer house, but Leo said he didn't feel the cold and Max took after him. Max got better. He too was in the habit of obedience. And up they all came in Camillo's Mercedes, the boot packed with wine and whisky.

And then the snow began. It came first in great, white, slow flakes from a dull sky, and then changed its nature: it became small and mean and a wind got up and we were in a blizzard, whited out. The gale would lift the snow from one field and plonk it down in another. The drifts were immense, the roads impassable.

Max, Polix, Camillo and Antigonus – and now Paulina too, for Leo wrote in a part for her, at Antigonus' insistence – scarcely registered the force and power of the blizzard, or its inconvenience. What better place was there to be but here, amongst friends? Cold? who cared? Whisky inured them to it. I was breast-feeding so could not indulge. I began to feel left out, nothing but the drudge. *Red at Night* occupied their thoughts, their dreams: ideas flew between them like humming birds, bright and swift. Never had so much creativity gone into what was, frankly, a rather trite thriller. I knew: I'd read it while Leo slept, massive snores shaking ancient roof timbers. Leo was an uneven writer, and not good at judging his own work. This was not his best.

The great snow, the great row. They go together in my mind. On the night in question, Leo came into my bedroom after midnight, very drunk. The last climactic scenes had been written: celebratory champagne had been added to whisky. He found me in my woolly dressing gown, hair loose, bent over the first twenty pages of a manuscript. I had been secretly writing. Worse, Polix was bent over too, whispering into my ear. I did not know which was the worse crime: secret writing or an apparent assignation with a man. I told

Leo I was asking Polix's advice about the opening pages of a stage play I was writing. Its name was *Perdita*. I was not believed. Leo's reaction was extreme.

He gave me a blow concomitant with his size – I am quite a little thing – and accused me of having it off with Polix. Under his nose, behind his back, his co-writer, he might have known. His rage was magnificent. I was quite flattered. He cared after all. Polix, the self-serving creep, cowered and apologised, I squealed – Leo had broken my ear-drum – Max woke up and screamed, Camillo and Antigonus came running. Paulina wisely kept to the safety of her room and the company of poltergeists.

Then Leo snatched up the manuscript of *Perdita* and ordered Camillo to take the manuscript – the entire first act, as it happened, not just the opening pages – and burn it, and Camillo, the miserable toe-rag, went off to do so. Leo, one hand wound round my hair and the other massive paw keeping both hands behind my back, led me to the dying log fire and I had to watch while flames devoured my creation. There was only the one copy. All these men and none of them did a thing to save me, so intent as they were on getting *Red at Night* off the ground. The fever of creativity devours common sense as easily as flames devour paper.

Oh the red blood reigned in the winter's pale, all right. Worse was to come. Leo laid about him with an axe. He could have been Jack Nicholson in *The Shining*. Doors splintered, sideboards split; we dodged, he chased. It was me he was after but no-one was safe. We hid in the pantry. Then Polix, Camillo, Antigonus and I decided our best bet was just to get out of there until Leo sobered up, and to take the *Red at Night* scripts with us in case in his madness he burned them too. Brave Paulina offered to stay behind to look after little Max. It was too cold for him out there in the night: his croup was returning.

We took the Mercedes. We had no snow chains. At first I thought that it was hopeless but the thaw had just begun. We pushed our way through slush. Polix was driving; I was in the passenger seat. All except me had been drinking. Like a wraith, a child came out of the snow, ran into the road. Polix braked and the car spun into the child. I heard the bump. I knew he was killed. The skid ended suddenly in a tree.

When I regained consciousness I was in the driving seat, and the police were all around. There was no sign of Polix, Camillo or Antigonus. They had scarpered. They had taken the scripts and left me to take the rap. I swore to the police that I had been the passenger but it suited them to believe I was the driver. The fact that I had never taken a driving test did not mean I could not drive. Leo was a power in these parts.

And it was Leo who swore in Court that I had been at the steering wheel, and alone in the car. I don't think he did it to punish me for having slept with Polix – we had been having an affair, actually, but how was Leo to know that? I could see Leo's reasoning. 'Either I lose my co-writer, my director, or my lead – or I lose my wife. It had better be my wife.' In the great world of the arts, wives and mothers are expendable. It is their duty to sacrifice themselves in the name of literature.

Now I'm not going to bore you with prison details. Prison is not nice. It is depressing and boring. It is demoralising. Worse for a woman than for a man. Friends and family shun you. To cause death by drunken driving is to be a pariah. My friend Paulina was the only visitor I had during all those years. But the authorities were sympathetic, gave me pen and paper, and allowed me to write. Leo might have destroyed the first act of my play but he could not destroy *Perdita*.

I knew every word by heart.

Meanwhile *Red at Night* went from strength to strength. Leo, Camillo and Paulina's husband Antigonus were the nation's darlings, thriving at my expense. My name was not mentioned in Bohemia Lodge: little Max grew up amongst its towers and battlements, its goblins and sprites, knowing nothing of his mother.

And as for me, I wrote and wrote, in between slopping out and de-lousing, and in five years had the complete manuscript. So long as no financial gain accrued to me I was allowed to send written work out of the prison. And so I sent my darling *Perdita*, child of my creativity, to face the perils of the outside world.

I sent her where I thought she would be safe, to Paulina. Now Paulina's marriage to Antigonus was on the rocks – fame and fortune had not dealt kindly with the great actor: he had taken to drink, drugs and whoring as the weak-minded will when faced with too much opportunity. He was on the verge of bankruptcy. Leo was bailing him out. Paulina showed Leo my play, thinking it would impress him, hoping it would make him relent and forgive me.

'See!' said innocent Paulina, 'How hard Hermione works, how much she suffers, is this not a creative genius in chains crying to be free?' It was the worst thing she could have done. Leo cunningly sent the play off to Antigonus, behind Paulina's back, with a view to him playing the lead, but knowing full well he would simply put it in his in-tray and forget all about it. Which was what happened. So there the manuscript moldered, unseen and forgotten.

Leo had the courtesy to send me a little note. 'Well done, darling. Paulina showed me. *Perdita* is a lovely piece of work. You always said you needed peace and quiet to write, and now you have it! Be happy.'

I suppose I am lucky Leo did not burn the manuscript. Sending it to Antigonus was the next best thing, and saved him from guilt.

Another Christmas: the red blood reigning in the winter's pale. This too I do not think about too much. A month to go before I was free. Little Max, daring to ask his father if I was dead, was told it was worse than that, I was in prison for murdering a little boy. Leo had been drinking that day: the blind rages were under control by doctor's prescription, but medication and alcohol combined to blur his judgement. The poor child ran out into the snowstorm, and in cruel repetition of that incident long ago, was knocked down and killed by a hit-and-run driver.

I was allowed to the funeral, in handcuffs. They were all there, Leo, Polix, Camillo, Antigonus – in their Armani suits and black ties, smooth and suave, crocodile tears flowing, paparazzi clicking and popping. They had just signed up for the fifth triumphant series of *Red at Night*.

The vicar quoted Shakespeare at the grave side, as the little coffin was lowered:

'What's gone and what's past help
Should be past grief.'

I didn't agree with that at all. Nothing is past grief.

Now I was out of prison, alone, without funds. Family and friends had cut me off. This is the plight of the female prisoner. There is precious little funding for their rehabilitation: the lion's share goes to the men. I went on the streets for a time. I was homeless, my son was dead, *Perdita* languishing forgotten: I could comfort myself in my heart that I was a better writer than Leo would ever be, but the knowledge didn't stop the paddling palms and pinching fingers that were now a feature of my life. Many of us have patches in our lives we are not proud of: this was one of mine.

But my play *Perdita*, my other child, had a life of its own. If art is the fruit of suffering, and I believe it is, and I had most certainly suffered, it was bound to come to something. None other than Polix's son Florizel came across the work, lying neglected, abandoned and unread on a shelf. Young Florizel, training at RADA, was doing work experience with Antigonus, archiving his press-cuttings and reviews: a dusty job and as it was to prove, a distressing one.

Antigonus had neglected to pay his VAT bill; he had simply failed to open envelopes or respond to their threats. The bailiffs broke into the house to reclaim Her Majesty's debt, as they are entitled to do, and pursuing him with their writs, found him finally in the attics, hanged by the neck, still swinging. Poor Antigonus, out of the plot. Exit, pursued by Vatman.

And Florizel read the play, loved it, and wanted to play the lead. He knew it would make his fame and fortune and so it did. He took *Perdita* to his father Polix, who recognised the work as mine, Hermione's, from so long ago, and went with it to Camillo. The passing years had worked their soothing magic upon even such ruthless men as they – or perhaps it simply was that with the death of Antigonus *Red at Night* had died as well. They had nothing to lose. Now, in *Perdita*, they could see a new future.

Their minions searched the back alleys of the city and I was found, washed, coiffed, restored, made much of. No one apologised: they expected me to be grateful. And so, such is the nature of women, I was.

Leo was kept uninformed: he was holed up in Bohemia Lodge, writing his autobiography, *The Sadness of Fame*. Central heating had been installed. *Perdita* went on in a nice little theatre in Newbury, Berkshire called the Water Mill, and the critics loved it. It transferred to the West End. Overnight I was famous, applauded, my time had come. Leo turned up, of course he did, well, his time was over and he knew it. I was of the new world, he of the old. He was prepared to bask in my glory, it paid so well. He wanted me back, to comfort him in his old age, and today's Leo is much comforted by Viagra.

And do you know, I went back? I forgave him. Because after all it was all for art and as Shakespeare said when we write we go to undreamed waters, unknown shores, and must expect to. Writing is a dangerous business.

And by the way, Camillo married the widowed Paulina. Leo told him to.

An Arrangement in Grey and Black

Deborah Moggach

Deborah Moggach's parents were both writers and she grew up 'to the sound of typewriters tapping on the veranda'. After graduating from Bristol University, Deborah worked in publishing for a few years and then lived in Pakistan for two years in the mid-1970s. It was there that she started writing and her first novel, *You Must Be Sisters*, was published in 1980. Since then she has written sixteen novels and two collections of short stories. Her latest novel is *In the Dark*. Deborah has two grown-up children and lives in London.

Whistler's mother says to him, 'I don't want to be *An Arrangement in Grey and Black, Number One*. I'm your mother.'

'Sit still.'

'And *Number One*! Are you expecting to have any more mothers?'

Whistler shakes his head. 'Only more paintings. Stop looking at me.'

'You have a strange expression on your face.'

'I'm just looking at you.'

'Not like a son, you're not. You're looking at an arrangement of me.'

'I'm looking at your soul.'

'Rubbish!' says his mother. 'My goodness, this chair's hard.'

'Stop complaining. I did let you sit down, didn't I?'

'Only because I nearly fainted. I'm sixty-seven, you know.'

'Turn back, Ma! I'm painting your profile.'

Deborah Moggach

'I know why you're painting my profile,' she replies. 'So you don't have to look at me.'

'I am looking at you.'

'So you don't have to face me.'

'Mother!'

There is a silence. Just the stroke, the loving stroke, of brush upon canvas. Outside the Thames flows, the waves stroking the bank. Then Whistler's mother speaks again.

'This nice wall behind me, nice patterned wallpaper, you've painted it grey, haven't you?'

'How do you know?'

'You think I don't know you?'

'You don't know anything about painting.'

'But I know you. Nobody will know you, son, better than I know you. Women will come and go, that woman you call The White Girl . . .'

'Oh oh, here we go . . .'

'Don't think I don't know about her, just because you get her out of the house when I'm here. Do you know what really rankles? Apart from your living in sinful concubinage. . .'

'Mother . . .'

' . . . apart from the fact that she's an inferior class, the shame of it, flaunting her around London . . . you know what really rankles? That when you paint her you call her a *White Girl* and me, you call me an *Arrangement*! *She's* the one who's an arrangement, and a shameful one at that.'

'She's an arrangement too, when I'm painting her. She's not Joanna Hiffernan . . .'

'Don't mention that name . . .'

'And as for our arrangement, she perfectly understands that I'm an artist . . .'

'Doesn't she want to get married?, asks his mother. 'Doesn't she want to have children?'

'The enemy of art, Mother, is the pram in the hallway.'

'But you were in a pram once. You are my son. Without me, you wouldn't be here.'

'So I'm your creation. You produced me and I'm producing this painting. And if you're interested, it's going very well.'

Whistler strokes the grey paint across the canvas. It isn't grey, of course. His mother doesn't understand about painting. So many pigments are laid on his palette – umber, indigo, green. He mixes them to create the most vibrant of greys. The wall behind his mother is as alive as she is. He says, 'You've been a good mother, Mother. That is your work. Mine is painting. In fact I will have children, here and there . . .'

'Here and there! What are they, litter?'

'Unlike you, however, I'll be a poor parent.'

'How? What will you do?'

'Nothing,' he replies. 'That's the point. I'll

shamefully neglect them, my future biographers won't even know how many there are, they won't be printed in the index.'

'How can you talk like that?'

'Because I'm an artist.'

'Stuff and nonsense!' she snorts. 'That's no excuse for being a bad parent.'

'You have to choose.'

'You won't even paint them? You won't even make them into an arrangement?'

Whistler shakes his head. 'They'll be irrelevant.'

'That's a terrible thing to say.'

Whistler doesn't reply. For a while he paints, in silence. Outside the window, across the gardens of Cheyne Walk, the river Thames runs glintingly in the sunshine. All is quiet, but for the admonishing slap, slap of its water against the bank. No road has yet been built, no cars and lorries thunder past, filling this room with exhaust fumes. It's 1871. As Whistler paints, his unborn children have yet to experience their sadness.

'I'm a selfish person, Mother.'

'Is that my fault?'

'I'm not blaming you. I'm no longer your responsibility.'

'I can't stop being a parent,' she replies. 'You're a grown man but it doesn't stop. When you were little I worried, oh how I worried. I worried you would die in infancy, like your brother Kirk and your brother Charlie. I worried that you'd be run over by a tram . . .'

'Now do you understand why I don't want to be a parent?'

'And still I worry . . .'

'Don't, Ma. I won't die for another thirty years.'

'Really?'

'Sit still and relax,' he says.

She gazes at him. 'What do you mean, you're a selfish person?'

'It's irrelevant. Only my work is important.'

'I thought I brought you up properly. To be a good Christian, to observe the Sabbath, to say your prayers . . .'

'You did your best, Mother, but I'm an artist and all artists are selfish. They have to be, to get their work done.'

'Rubbish.'

'I'm ruthless, I'm vain. Know how vain? One of my fans, they told me, "*There are only two great painters, you and Velasquez*," and I replied "*Why drag in Velasquez?*" I'll become increasingly touchy and litigious. When Ruskin criticises my painting *Nocturne in Black and Gold*, know what he'll say? I haven't even painted it yet and already he's sharpening his knife. He'll say *I never expected to hear a coxcomb ask two hundred guineas for flinging a pot of paint in the public's face.* That's what he'll say, and as God's my witness I'll drag him through the courts.'

'Why?'

'Because I must defend my art.'

Whistler's mother, who can no longer face her son, stares into the middle distance. 'And how will you behave in your private life?'

'Abominably. But what concern is that of anybody?'

'It concerns *me.*'

'But who will know or care? It's this that matters. This you.'

'This arrangement?' She shifts in her seat. 'Oh, my back's killing me.'

'I care nothing for the past, present or future. I care for harmony.'

'Why will you quarrel with everybody then?'

' . . . harmony of line and colour,' says Whistler.

'If the present doesn't matter, why will you spend your time quarrelling with the critics?'

' . . . that's the harmony which will outline us all. In 1881 you'll die, in Hastings . . .'

She turns to face him, startled. 'How do you know?'

'Turn back. How do I know? Because this painting releases me from the here and now. You will die, but the true you . . .'

'The arrangement of me . . .'

'You'll be sent to America. Over the next nineteen years you'll be exhibited in London, Philadelphia, New York, Paris, Dublin, Munich and Amsterdam.'

'I've never been to Amsterdam.'

'You will.'

'Or Dublin.' She pauses. 'Or Munich.'

'You'll finally be sold to the French and can you guess where you'll end up?'

'In the cemetery.'

'In the Louvre,' says Whistler. 'I'll sell you to the French, where you'll become one of the most famous portraits of all time, as famous as Leonardo's immortal *Mona Lisa*. *The Cornhill Magazine* will call me an amazing natural genius. They'll say the qualities of feeling are irresistible . . .'

'I'm freezing. Can't you light the fire?'

'They'll say that *nothing can be truer than the patient fold of the aged hands and the pathetic calm of the aged face* . . .'

'Pathetic?' she snaps.

His voice rises. 'This is the painting with which I'll be remembered, and with which you'll be remembered too! When you and I are in the past, *this* you, she'll always be in the present tense.'

'She is me, you know.'

'This painting releases you from the here and now . . . from this house in Chelsea, from your pride and disappointment in me, from my own bad behaviour. None of it will matter because before too long it will all be over.'

'What about the casualties? Your children, your broken friendships, the woman with whom you live and for whom I'm feeling increasingly sorry?'

'She will be *The White Girl* and hang in the Washington National Gallery. People will gaze at her as they gaze on you, and none of this will matter. You lost children to death and I lost children to art, but none of it will matter. Do you understand?'

There is a long silence. Whistler's mother wants to turn, to look at him, but she keeps her head in profile. She feels her son gazing at her – not at her, at *her* – her white mop cap, her determined chin, the folds of her dress – as he stands at his easel. He is a blur, in the corner of her eye. Today he is not a blurred son. He is a blurred artist. She is an arrangement but she too must re-arrange her thoughts. *Stuff and nonsense*, she said, but now she is pausing to consider. There is plenty of time to think, sitting here on this chair that seems to grow harder by the minute. Her children have been her chink into the future, her own immortality, but that is something her son cannot understand. The way he works is different. A busy stir in the corner of her eye, he is busy making her immortal. *You will always be in the present tense.*

At last he puts down his brush and lights a cigarette. 'It's finished,' he says. 'Come and have a look at yourself.'

She gets up creakingly – her back, her joints! She walks over and looks at the painting.

'Forget children,' he murmurs. 'Forget reproduction. You will be reproduced, Mother dear, for as long as such things will be possible . . .'

★ ★ ★

The river flows, glinting in the changing light of the seasons. Its current chases the years and neither of them catches up with each other. Years pass. Only the Thames remains unchanged as London grows taller around it. A hundred years pass. Whistler's children, who have entered and left the world unrecorded, are long since dead. Opposite Cheyne Walk the office blocks have risen and traffic thunders along the Embankment.

Behind the office blocks, in Stockwell, a painter is struggling with her own arrangement. It is a collage. It consists of blown-up photographs of art critics and over their mouths she has stuck sticking plasters – the transparent ones, with just a small oblong in the middle to staunch the wound. The artist's name is Susannah. She is having doubts about it, now it is finished. She stands back, pushing her fingers

41

through her cropped hair. Is its target too small and petty? Should she be helping her daughter with her homework?

For Susannah has a daughter, Blythe, who is fourteen. Blythe is sitting in her bedroom struggling with an essay on *Animal Farm*. Outside the church bells ring. It's Sunday and they are calling whoever is left, whoever still believes in such things, to worship. Susannah has never taken her daughter to church. She has given her no father figure, transubstantial or temporal. Blythe's father decamped at her birth and was last spotted on the beach in Goa, dispensing drugs. Susannah has brought up her daughter alone. She has farmed her out to childminders whilst she has travelled around making video installations. For several years she has had her doubts about her own abilities both as an artist and as a mother, for in trying to cope with both of these she feels she has succeeded in neither.

Susannah gazes at her collage. Way beyond her twelfth-floor window the Thames flows unperturbed. How many artists have painted this river, which has shown a fine disregard both for them and their critics? Who cares, anyway, what the critics say? Susannah has read a book on Turner. *The Literary Gazette*, in 1842, described his work thus: '*His paintings are produced as if by throwing handfuls of white and blue and red at the canvas, letting what chanced to stick, stick.*'

She looks at the sticking plasters. In the months ahead the adhesive will dry and they will fall off like scabs. Beneath, maybe the wounds will have healed, for what is this painting and does it really matter? Was it worth snapping at her daughter?

Susannah is thinking this when the door opens. Blythe comes in, holding a bunch of chrysanthemums. 'Happy Mother's Day,' she says.

'Is it?' Susannah jumps up and takes them. 'I forgot.'

Blythe gives her an envelope. Susannah pulls out a card.

She gazes at the painting. She gazes at the profile, stark and compromising against the grey wall. *An Arrangement in Grey and Black: Portrait of the Artist's Mother.*

'I know it's a bit gloomy,' says her daughter. 'But the others were really, like, soppy.'

'Are you trying to tell me something?' asks Susannah. 'Should I have been like this, sitting here forever, never going away?'

Her daughter shakes her head. 'I'm not trying to tell you anything.' She looks at the card. 'It's just Art, innit?'

Mother and Daughters

Lesley Pearse

Lesley Pearse was born in Rochester, Kent, but flat-shared in London throughout the Swinging Sixties where she worked in promotions and had a brief spell as a Bunny girl at the Playboy Club. She has lived in the West Country for the last thirty three years, and has three daughters and a grandson. She is President of the Bath and West Wiltshire NSPCC, a charity very close to her heart, and she is the author of seventeen bestselling books, the latest being *Gypsy*, published by Penguin.

'So what is your issue with your girls, then?' Avril asked curiously, filling up my wine glass again. 'You seem angry with them.'

I'd come over to her house for lunch, and I suppose the good food, wine and being cosseted by Avril must have lulled me into having a bit of a whinge.

'It's hardly an issue, and I'm not angry, only weary,' I replied. 'I just think that girls in their late twenties with homes of their own should be self-sufficient.'

'Surely they don't expect you to provide for them?' Avril's perfectly made-up eyes opened very wide.

I wish I'd remained my usual tight-lipped self, for Avril adores a drama and she can easily whip up the most minor of irritations into one. We may have been friends for twenty years but to be honest our only common ground is that our children are the same age.

She's got a dynamic husband and doesn't choose to work, a gorgeous well-organised home and two boys who've never given her a moment's grief. Well, not that she's ever admitted to!

I, on the other hand, am divorced, work and live in my chaotic terraced house, which no glossy magazine would ever want to feature, and over the years Lauren and Alice have contributed to turning my hair white.

'Oh no, they don't come to me for money,' I said quickly. They have in the past, but I'm not admitting that. 'It's not about money or wanting stuff. I'm just tired of being leaned on. They ring to bleat on about their boyfriends, ask me how to make a curry, the postcode for their godmother, anything and everything. Only yesterday Lauren rang to ask me her father's birthday, and whether she should wash cashmere or have it dry cleaned. I ask you! Can't she get a birthday book like anyone else, or read the washing instructions on the garment?'

'They are dependent on you because you encourage it,' Avril replied smugly. 'When Miles and Grant were eighteen, I bought them a Filofax. I put all the family birthdays and addresses in them so they would never need to come back to me for that information.'

'Do they actually send a card to anyone?' I asked curiously. I couldn't imagine it, they seemed very detached and cool young men.

'I wouldn't know,' she said crisply. 'They have such busy lives.'

In a flash of intuition I realised that Miles and Grant don't bother much with her, and I'd been tactless enough to whinge on about my girls pestering me too much.

'It isn't just the girls who lean on me, it's everyone,' I said. This was true, but I was trying to drop my daughters out of the equation. 'I actually dream of having a whole week when absolutely no one makes any demands on me. No advice wanted, no counselling required, nothing. I bet I'd get an extra couple of hours in each day if no one rang or called round.'

Maybe I was exaggerating a little, but there's no doubt I'm seen as a soft touch and a fount of all knowledge. The trouble is just lately all this leaning on me is beginning to make me sag under the weight.

'Then you must go somewhere to unwind,' Avril said, and her tone suggested she had lost interest in my problems. 'How about the Bahamas? Gerald and I had such a relaxing time there.'

That of course led her into getting out the photos and I had to admire the fabulous suite, the empty pristine beach complete with waving palm trees and at least three dozen pictures of Avril in different beautifully coordinated outfits. There was only one picture of her husband Gerald, very Hemingway-ish in a cream linen jacket and Panama hat. I wonder if she ever appreciates that her swish lifestyle is all down to his brains and hard work.

It was around five when the taxi came to take me home. I glanced round at Avril waving goodbye on the doorstep and felt a pang of envy. She looked lovely. Slender because she watches what she eats and goes to a gym, her shoulder-length blonde hair artfully put up, yet giving the impression she'd just scooped it up in the glitzy comb at the last minute. A silver-grey silk tunic and matching pants, even her necklace, a festoon of large grey, pink-and-white pearls, probably cost a king's ransom.

I'm a bit plump, so I opt for black loose-fitting clothes and interesting beads to jazz things up. I could definitely do with going to the hairdresser more often to keep the grey hair at bay. My girls tell me I don't look forty-nine, and that I haven't got a line on my face, but they're just being kind.

But it wasn't Avril's glamour or wealth that I was envious of, nor even the Georgian house with its matching potted bay trees flanking the glossy front door. It was her serenity.

We met through mutual friends at a barbeque in Islington. Lauren was eight, Alice seven and they ganged up with Miles and Grant who were also there. Even then there was a huge disparity between our two families. The boys went to a private school, mine to the local primary. Jeff, my husband, was a plumber, and Gerald was a high flyer in the city. Avril and I were thrown together because our children liked each other, but I think it developed into friendship just because we were so different. I enjoyed having a posh and glamorous friend, and she liked having someone in her life she didn't have to compete with.

When the children got to fourteen and fifteen they no longer wanted to socialise outside their own little clique at their schools, but Avril and I remained friends. I split up with Jeff and started my soft-furnishing business, and Avril got all her friends and acquaintances to come to me for their curtains, blinds and cushions.

She was always saying that I should open a showroom, advertise myself as an interior designer and employ other people to do the work. But I was happy working at home, cutting the curtains out on the dining room table, I wanted to be there when the girls got back from school.

I'm still happy working there. Granted I have had an extension built which is now my workshop, and I also have two women working for me, but I still see it as something of a cottage industry. Fortunately a successful one!

But sadly I don't have serenity. Exacting

customers, deadlines to meet, problems with fabric suppliers and far too much going on all around me rules that out. Even the snootiest customers feel they can burden me with their problems. You can't be serene when you lie awake worrying whether the pale pink silk you recommended for some festoon blinds, might just end up looking like a pair of frilly knickers. Or ignore the three a.m. panics that the measurements you took earlier in the day might be wrong. Then there are the girls wanting to share every part of their lives with me.

I love them to pieces, but I am guilty of wishing they'd get married to men who will whisk them off to live in Australia or South Africa. Then I'd be invited for just a two-week holiday once a year, and I could be so happy watching my rich and handsome sons-in-law shouldering all my girl's mundane problems.

But up till now the men in their lives have also adopted me as the Ever-Listening Ear. Often they even come to see me after they've been dumped. I just can't seem to shake people off.

When I arrived home the dogs greeted me with their usual enthusiasm. They both started life as Must-Have fashion statement for my daughters, but then were passed on to me when there were too many puddles and chewed shoes.

'I'll change my shoes and then I'll take you to the

park,' I told them, then pressed the button on the answer phone to listen to my messages.

I groaned as I listened. Mrs Selbright hoped I might be able to finish her new curtains by the end of the month because she's got family coming over from America. Mr Johnston was querying my estimate; he couldn't believe any fabric cost £35 a metre. Madge Downes, a particularly good customer, had rung me to tell me she was out of hospital following her hysterectomy and hoped I might pop in for a chat.

It was tempting to ring Mrs Selbright and suggest she come down here and hand stitch her own curtains if she wants them any quicker. Mr Johnston deserved to be shown the invoice for his next-door neighbour's curtains which cost £65 a metre. But I couldn't help feeling for Madge. She was a lovely lady and clearly her cold-hearted family didn't appreciate that a woman who has had her womb removed needs a bit of T L C.

As I sat down and took off my new red killer heels and massaged some blood back into my aching feet (I had thought Avril would be impressed by them, but she didn't even notice), it struck me what a mess the house was. I'm kind of stuck in an eighties' time warp, with stripped pine, Laura Ashley prints and far too many knick-knacks. Once I thought it the perfect décor for a Victorian house.

But today it looks like me – tired, shabby and in need of a facelift. As a re-vamper of other people's houses I haven't got the time or energy for my own. The curtain pole had come adrift in the bay window; one tweak of the curtains and the whole lot would come down. The brown stain on the pale blue carpet seemed to be creeping out from under the rug I had covered it with too. I didn't even want to think about the horrors in the kitchen; last time Lauren was home she remarked that I must be the only person left in England with wood-effect Formica.

In the park half an hour later, wearing flat comfy shoes and watching the dogs sniff every tree trunk, I felt less edgy. I decided I would take the phone off the hook for the evening and go to work on Mrs Selbright's curtains. I'd get one of my employees to phone Mr Johnston first thing in the morning, and I would go and see Madge for an hour and take her some flowers.

I idly thought that maybe I should order a skip and dump almost thirty years of accumulated clutter from my lounge into it. It would be so good to start from scratch again, and create a room just for me. I found myself daydreaming of turquoise and parchment white, with raspberry accents here and there. I saw myself lying on a gorgeous soft cream sofa, wearing a pale-pink negligée and matching fluffy mules.

I was so busy with this happy daydream, I forgot to put the dogs back on their leads well before I got back to the low wall that surrounds the park. A few years earlier I made this mistake, and Fred, the boisterous one, bolted for home and almost got himself run over.

I came out of my reverie to find I was just twenty yards from the wall and Fred had jumped up on it.

'Come here, Fred!' I said sharply.

Bert, the quieter one, barked as if to point out he was a good boy. 'Stay!' I ordered him and advanced on Fred with the lead.

But before I could reach him, Fred had leapt off straight across the road. The road by the park has very little traffic, but Fred was already heading towards the busier street just around the corner.

'Stay!' I yelled, and darted out between two parked cars to reach him.

I don't know why I didn't hear or see the car coming but I didn't hear its brakes squeal until it hit me.

There were some hazy memories: a feeling I was tossed up in the air, then crashed down hard. And a man kneeling beside me speaking, but that was all.

They told me much later at the hospital that I was unconscious when the ambulance arrived. I could hardly be surprised at that, for my right leg hurt like hell and every other part of me ached or stung.

Miraculously, the only thing broken was my leg,

and I'd sprained my wrist. The rest of the injuries were fairly superficial, just nasty gravel grazes on my cheeks, arms and legs. It seemed I was lucky that the driver of the car was going quite slowly looking for somewhere to park when I ran out into his path. The nurse said if he'd been going faster I might have been killed.

The driver of the car was also something of a Good Samaritan too, for aside from calling the ambulance, he noticed the dogs' leads which I'd dropped, and as the dogs came over to me lying in the road, he put them back on and held them.

I was about to panic about the dogs, but the nurse informed me the police had discovered where I lived, and they'd called on Sally, my next-door neighbour. She, bless her, had volunteered to take care of the dogs, and gave the police Lauren's and Alice's telephone numbers.

I felt very sorry for myself that night. After the X-rays, which revealed a clean break in my lower leg, they cleaned me up, put my leg in plaster, and my wrist in a sling. But because I'd lost consciousness, they had to keep me in to check for brain damage.

I was fairly certain my brain was fine, or why else would I be worrying how I was going to work, walk the dogs, clean the house and do all the million and one other jobs I had to do? As far as I knew, broken legs took weeks to mend, especially when you weren't in the first flush of youth.

It was well after eleven before I got taken to a ward, and all the other patients appeared to be asleep. 'Your daughter Lauren called,' a young nurse told me. 'She said to tell you she and Alice are at your house and they've got the dogs back. They wanted to come and see you tonight, but I said it would be better to wait till tomorrow. And they sent their love.'

I was tearful by then. 'How am I going to manage?' I asked her.

'I'm sure your daughters will take care of you,' she replied. 'You try to go to sleep now. Everything will be ok.'

I didn't believe the girls would take care of me. How could they? They could barely take care of themselves.

I did sleep; whatever it was they gave me even wiped out the pain in my leg for a few hours. The girls came in at ten in the morning. When they saw my grazed face, sling and plastered leg, their eyes filled with tears.

Even if I am biased, they are remarkably pretty girls. Lauren is dark-haired, as I used to be, with soulful eyes and high cheekbones. She goes in for the tailored look, dark suits and crisp white shirts. Alice has light-brown hair, but I haven't seen that in years. At that moment it was streaked blond. Alice was into girly stuff, pink fluffy jumpers, big blingy belts round her skinny jeans. She's a giggler, while Lauren is more serious.

'What were you thinking of, Mum?' Alice reproached me. 'Running out in front of a car! You could've been killed. What would we have done without you?'

'Learned to look after yourselves?' I retorted unnecessarily harshly.

I felt ashamed when Lauren produced some clean clothes for me. She'd even had the sense to pick out the baggiest linen trousers to go over the plaster. Furthermore she proceeded to dress me as if I was the child.

I burst into tears then because I suddenly saw that I really couldn't do much for myself.

'Don't cry, Mummy,' Alice said. She hadn't called me that since she was six. 'We're going to take care of you. We told Mavis and Ruth in the workroom to carry on with whatever jobs were most urgent. We said we'd ring round anyone else when we get back. You're just going to put your feet up on the sofa and let your leg heal.'

It's weird doing nothing when you've spent your whole life rushing about. That first day I dozed a lot, and I hurt too much to want to move. I vaguely heard the girls' laughter out in the hall; it seemed they were trying out the crutches that had been delivered for me. But they didn't let me try them;

when I wanted to go to the loo, they supported me while I hopped there on my good leg. They brought me meals on a tray, gave me magazines to read, and later that evening they undressed me and helped me into my bed.

By the second day of being home I wasn't in so much pain, and I started to worry again. Not so much about what was going on in the workroom, Mavis and Ruth are as capable as I am, and they would get the outstanding jobs finished on time, even if it meant having to stay later.

It was my daughters I was worried about.

Lauren works for an advertising agency and Alice is a dental nurse. They might think it was great to have a couple of days off to play nurse. Cooking, cleaning and walking the dogs might seem like fun at first, especially as they don't usually spend much time together. But that would soon wear off and they'd start squabbling.

I was on my feet, having a go with the crutches, when they came in and caught me.

'You aren't ready for that yet,' Lauren said bossily. She took my arm and lowered me back onto the sofa.

'I've got the whole series of "Absolutely Fabulous" for you to watch,' Alice chimed in. 'Now just behave yourself. We'll decide when you can start hopping around.'

'But I can't impose on you two,' I argued. 'You

should be at work and you've got homes of your own.'

'We've got it all worked out,' Lauren said. 'I'm going to work on Monday and Tuesdays, and Alice is going in for the rest of the week. But we're both going to stay at nights until we are sure you can manage. Don't even think of arguing with us.'

'But you'll get fed up,' I retorted weakly.

They looked at one another and smirked.

'Has it occurred to you that we just might want to do something for you?' Lauren exclaimed. 'All we ever do is lean on you. This is our chance to show our appreciation for all you've done for us over the years. And we actually like you, Mum, as well as loving you. So it's no chore being here.'

I was too stunned to say anything more.

I saw stuff in the subsequent days which I could scarcely believe. Alice going out with my box of tools and a set of finished curtains. Not just to hang them at the client's home, but to fix up new curtain poles. I got a jubilant call later from the client saying how wonderful they were, and how efficient and tidy she was.

'How did you know how to do it?' I asked in wonder.

Alice just shrugged and said she'd seen me do it often enough and practised in her own flat.

Lauren answered the phone, and explained my circumstances, adding she could go to their home to measure up and take them fabric sample books.

But the way they were helping with my business was nothing to the things they did for me personally. Lauren dyed my hair, she tidied up cupboards and threw out stuff I didn't want, and did my VAT return. Alice did most of the cooking, and made huge quantities, putting some of it in small pots to freeze, so when they left I'd have no need to cook. She spring-cleaned everywhere, even tackled the workshop one evening when Mavis and Ruth had gone.

Suddenly there was order where once there had been chaos, and in the evenings the three of us sat with fabric swatches and paint charts and discussed doing up the house. The girls knew men who could do the work, and even costed it all out for me.

'We'll organise it all for August,' Lauren said firmly. 'Mavis and Ruth are away then and your plaster will be off. Alice is going to take you away for a week, but I'll stay here to move stuff, bully the men and take care of the dogs.'

I had to fight back tears of sheer joy. Not because of the holiday or having my house done up, but because the girls I thought were dizzy and a bit self-centred, had become caring, confident and capable adults. That's really all a mother needs to assure her she's done a good job.

'It's a shame you had to get run over for us to

realise how much we took you for granted,' Alice said in a small voice as we admired the newly decorated lounge.

We'd just got back from Malta, memories of being stressed and weeks of a leg in plaster had been wiped out by sunshine and happiness. But to find the lounge a pristine, cream blank canvas, awaiting the delivery of a new carpet and sofa, that was sheer joy.

I turned to Alice and cupped her pretty face in my hands. 'It's a shame too I had to be run over to see what strong, kind women you and Lauren have become.'

'Come and look at this, Mum!' Lauren called out.

I followed her voice out into the kitchen, and when I saw it my mouth fell open in shock. The old fake wood Formica was gone; in its place were dove grey cupboards and a shiny beech work surface.

'They are the same old carcasses, we just got new doors and painted them,' Lauren said. 'But as we were taking off the old work surface, we chucked out the horrible old sink while we were at it.'

'I bathed you in that sink,' I said, laughing as I remembered them as babies sitting up there splashing around as I made the tea. 'If anyone had told me then that one day you two would re-vamp this place for me, I would never have believed it.'

That evening, as we shared one last takeaway before the girls went back to their own homes, I suddenly had one of those blinding flashes of revelation. By letting the girls see me vulnerable and in need of help, I'd given them something far more valuable than all the presents, advice and the time I'd given them in the past. Through allowing them to do things for me, our relationship was balanced now. Along with being mother and daughters, we were friends.

I tried to express this, but I don't think they really understood that I was trying to say something far more than a thank-you.

'Just don't fill the house with clutter again,' Lauren said reprovingly.

'And stop taking on the worries of the world,' Alice chipped in.

I smiled. I had never felt this serene, ever. It felt good.

The Tipping Point

Helen Simpson

Helen Simpson is the author of four collections of short stories – *Four Bare Legs in a Bed*, *Dear George*, *Hey Yeah Right Get a Life*, and *Constitutional*. She was chosen as one of Granta's twenty Best of Young British Novelists and has won the Sunday Times Young Writer of the Year Award, the Somerset Maugham Award, the Hawthornden Prize and the E.M.Forster Award. She lives in London with her husband and two children.

Look at that sky. It's almost sitting on the windscreen. Whose idea was it to hold the Summer School up in the wilds this year? I know my sweet Americans would follow me to the ends of the earth for my thoughts on the Bard; and I know Stratford venues are stratospheric these days. But all this way to study the Scottish play *in situ* smacks of desperation. If ever a sky looked daggers, this is it.

I was quite looking forward to the drive, actually. Impossible to get lost, my esteemed colleague Malkie MacNeil told me, just follow the A82 all the way and enjoy the scenery, the mountains, best in the world, blah blah. So I left Glasgow reasonably bright and hopeful this morning after a dish of porridge, up along Loch Lomond, and the light has drained steadily away through Tarbet, Ardlui, Tyndrum, until I realise that it's eleven in the morning on the fifth of August and I've got to turn on the headlights. Storm clouds over Glen Coe. 'The cloud-capp'd Towers, the gorgeous Palaces.' Not really. More like a celestial housing estate.

Alright, let's have something suitably gloomy in the way of music. Here we are. *Winterreise* with Dietrich Fischer-Dieskau and his manly baritone. No finer example of the pathetic fallacy than Schubert's *Winterreise* 'What's that when it's at home, Dr Beauman?' That is the reading of one's own emotion into external nature, child. I still cannot believe that I, confirmed commitmentphobe, have been cast as the rejected lover, ignominiously dumped like some soppy First Year.

Nun ist die Welt so trube, der Weg gehult in Schnee. My German may not be fluent but it's become more than passable in the last year. You'd allow that, Angelika? Now the world is so bleak, the path shrouded in snow. *Schnee.*

It was immediate. As soon as we first clapped eyes on each other etcetera. But, joking apart, it was. I was over in Munich to give my paper on *Milton's Comus: the Masque Form as Debate and Celebration*, mainly because I wanted to check out the painted rococo Cuvilliéstheater – crimson, ivory and gold – on Residenzstrasse. I needed it for my chapter on European Court Theatre, for the book which now bears your name as dedicatee.

You were in charge of that Conference, Head of Arts Admin for all the participating institutions that week.

Once it was over we went back to your flat in Cologne. Jens was staying with his grandmother as luck would have it. Beautiful Angelika, with your fierce pale eagle eyes and beaming smile. I remember capering round your bed like a satyr after you'd given me the first of your ecological curtain lectures. I was quoting Comus at you to shut you up:

Wherefore did nature pour her bounties forth
With such a full and unwithdrawing hand,
Covering the earth with odours, fruits and flocks,
Thronging the seas with spawn innumerable,
But all to please and sate the curious taste?

I was proud and stout and gleeful in the presence of your angularity. It felt like a challenge. Heaping you with good things became part of that. I filled your austere kitchen with delicacies, though that wasn't easy as you are of course vegan.

'Enough is enough,' you said, pushing me away.

'You can never have enough,' I laughed. 'Didn't you know that?'

'Not so. I have.'

Ich will den Boden kussen, / durdringen Eis und Schnee / mit meinen heiBen Tranen. Schnee again. I want to kiss the ground, to pierce the ice and snow with my hot tears. Yes, well. Romanticism was your besetting sin, Angelika; your quasi-mystical accusatory ecospeak about the planet. Whereas my

line is, if it's going to happen, it's going to happen –
I don't see how anything mankind does can impose
change on overwhelming natural phenomena like
hurricanes and tsunamis. We resemble those small
frail figures in a painting by Caspar David Friedrich,
dwarfed by the immensity of nature. You took me to
see his great painting *Das Eismeer* in the Hamburger
Kunsthalle, jagged ice floes in a seascape beyond
hope; and you used it as a jumping-off point to
harangue me about the collapse of the Larsen B ice
shelf. My clever intense passionate Angelika, so
quick to imagine the worst, and so capable of
anguish; you wept like a red-eyed banshee when you
gave me the push.

An ominous cloudscape, this, great weightless
barricades of cumulonimbus blocking the light. I can't
see another car or any sign of humanity. Once out of
this miserable valley, I'll stop for petrol in Ballachulish.
Then it's on up past Loch Linnhe, Loch Lochy, Loch
Oich, Loch Ness, and I'll be there. Inverness. What's
done is done. Half-way through the week there's a
day trip planned to Cawdor Castle, where Duncan
doubtless shakes his gory locks on mugs and
mousemats all over the gift shop.

So then I applied for a peripatetic fellowship at the
University of Cologne, and got it. I brushed up my
Schiller. I wrote a well-received paper on Gotthold
Ephraim Lessing's *Minna von Barnhelm* and gave a

seminar on Ödön von Horvath, the wandering playwright who all his life was terrified of being struck by lightning and then, during a Parisian thunderstorm, took shelter beneath a tree on the Champs Elysees and was killed by a falling branch. Let that be a warning to you, Angelika: you can worry too much.

We were very happy, you and me and Jens. He's unusually thoughtful and scrupulous, that boy; like his mother. They had their annual day of atonement at his school while I was over, when the children are instructed to consider the guilt of their militaristic forefathers in the last century. That was the night he had an asthma attack and we ended up in Casualty. Cue copious lectures from you on air quality, of course.

And here's the rain, driving against the windscreen with a violence fit to crack it. It's almost comic, this journey, the menace of those massed clouds, the grey-green gloom.

Nor do I have a residual belief that rain is in any way cleansing or purgative. No, no. As you so painstakingly taught me, Angelika, our sins of pollution lock into the clouds and come down as acid rain. Hence *waldsterben*, or forest death; and from *waldsterben* you would effortlessly segue into flash floods, storm surge, wildfire, drought, and on to carbon sequestration. You were not the only one. You and your friends discussed these things for hours, organising petitions, marching here and there. Your activism made my English students look like solipsistic children, their political concerns stretching with some effort to top-up fees and back down again to the price of hair straighteners.

You were in a constant state of alarm. I wanted you to talk about me, about you and me, but the apocalyptic *Zeitgeist* intruded.

Darling, shall we go for a swim? No, my love, for the oceans have warmed up and turned acidic. All plankton is doomed and, by association, all fish and other swimmers. Sweetheart, what can I do to melt your heart? Nothing, for you are indifferent to the ice albedo feedback; you are unconcerned that the planet's shield of snow, which reflects heat back into space, is defrosting. That our world grows dangerously green and brown, absorbing more heat than ever before, leaves you cold.

My own dear heart, let's make a happy future for ourselves, for you and me and Jens. How can that be when the world is melting and you don't care? How can we be *gemutlich* together in the knowledge that the twin poles of the world are dissolving, that permafrost is no longer permanent and will unloose vast clouds of methane gas to extinguish us all?

You did love me. You told me so. *Ich liebe dich.*

Then came your ultimatum. We couldn't go on seeing each other like this. Yes, you loved my flying visits, you loved being with me. But no, you could not bear it that our love was sustained at the expense of the future. By making it dependent on cut-price flights we were doing the single worst possible thing in our power as private individuals to harm the planet.

'Love miles,' I countered, morally righteous, fighting fire with fire.

'Selfish miles,' you retorted. 'We are destroying other people's lives when we do this.' Very truthful and severe you are, Angelika; very hard on yourself as well as others.

Time for a change of CD. More Schubert lieder, I think, but let's drop Fischer-Dieskau. He's a tad heavy-hearted for Scotland, a bit of a dampener where it's already damp enough. Ah, Gerard Souzay, he's my man. Rather an eccentric choice, but my father used to listen to him and I cottoned on to what he admired. A great voice, fresh, rich, essentially baritonal but keener on beauty than usual. Let's skip *Der Jungling und der Tod*, though. OK, here comes the Erlking. There's a boy here, too, riding on horseback through the night with his father, holding close to his father. Oh, it's a brilliant micro-opera, this song, one voice singing four parts – narrator, father, boy, and the lethal wheedling Erlking. I'd forgotten how boldly elliptical it is, and how infectious the boy's terror: '*Mein Vater, mein Vater, und horest du nicht,/ Was Erlkonig mir leise verspricht?*' My father, my father, and don't you hear/

the Erlking whispering promises to me? But his father can't hear anything, can't see anything, only the wind and the trees.

I used to start laughing uncontrollably at this point, which annoyed *my* father, who was trying to listen; but it appealed to my puerile sense of humour – vater as farter.

Mein Vater, mein Vater, jetzt fasst er mich an!
Erlkonig hat mir ein Leids getan!

My father, my father, now he is taking hold of me! The Erlking has hurt me! And by the time the father has reached home the boy lies dead in his arms. *Tot.*

Listen, Angelika. You make my blood boil. What possible difference can it make whether I get on a plane or not? The plane will take off regardless. Why don't you concentrate your energies on all those herds of farting cattle, eh? All those cows and sheep farting and belching. Then after that you could get the rainforests under control! The blazing forests! You don't want me.

It's stopped raining at last. I can see ahead again, the air is clearer now. A truly theatrical spectacle, this sky, with its constant changes of scene. I couldn't do it in the end. I wanted tenure, sure, but I was being asked to give up too much. The world. The world well lost? No. No, no, not even for you, Angelika.

In September I'm attending a weekend conference on Performance Art at the University of

Uppsala in Sweden. I'm not going by coach. There's a seminar on *Storm und Drang* in Tokyo this autumn, as well as my Cardiff-based sister's wedding party in Seville. After that there's an invitation to the Sydney Festival to promote my new book, and the usual theatre conference at Berkeley in spring. All paid for, of course, except the return ticket to Seville, which cost me precisely £11 – just about manageable even on an academic's meagre stipend.

You used to have to join the Foreign Office if you wanted to travel on anything like this scale. Now everybody's at it. The budget airlines arrived and life changed overnight.

Sorry, but it's true. The world's our sweetshop. We've got used to it, we want it; there's no going back.

The downside is, I lost my love. She followed through. And how. She caused us both enormous pain. Ah, come on! For all I know she's got back together with that little *dramaturg* from Bremen, the one with the tiny hands and feet. So?

Look at those schmaltzy sunbeams backlighting the big grey cloud. Perfect scenery for the arrival of a *deus ex machina*. 'What's that when it's at home, Dr Beauman?' A far-fetched plot device to make everything alright again, my dear. There's Ballachulish in the distance. A painted god in a cardboard chariot. An unlikely happy ending, in other words.

A Dress to Die For

Isabel Wolff

Isabel Wolff read English at Cambridge and was a broadcaster and journalist before becoming a full-time novelist. She has written seven bestselling romantic comedies including *Rescuing Rose*, *A Question of Love* and *Forget Me Not*. Her eighth novel, *A Vintage Affair*, will be published by HarperCollins early in 2009. Isabel lives in London with her partner and their two young children and in her spare time enjoys playing in the sandpit and going down the slide. For more information visit www.IsabelWolff.com

It's been a year now since I opened Flashback, my vintage dress shop. Before that I had a stall on Portobello but that was hard going, especially in the winter, having to haul the clothes in and out of the van on freezing dark mornings than standing around in the cold all day. So when a friend told me about a lease that was coming up on this site in Hampstead, I took a deep breath, decided to go for it and, so far, it's been a success. People seem to enjoy coming here – perhaps because the interior's modern and light and the clothes are well displayed with plenty of space between the hangers. So many vintage dress shops are a mess, with bags and shoes all over the place and the rails so crammed that you give yourself an upper body workout just going through them. Flashback isn't a bit like that – it's more like being somewhere nice, like Phase Eight. Then of course there are the clothes – a necessarily eclectic range from the flapper dresses of the twenties to the New Look suits of the fifties right through to the spangly bat-winged tops of the early eighties. My customers say that coming into Flashback is like entering Aladdin's cave.

People ask me what I like most about what I do, and, of course, a great part of it is the pleasure I get from working with garments that are so well made. These clothes haven't been churned out by the thousand in some faceless factory – they've been made with real craftsmanship, artistry and pride.

Take this midnight blue silk taffeta evening dress for example. It's by Balenciaga from about 1960. Look at the elegant simplicity of the cut, and the way the hem is slightly raised to reveal shoes. Look at the deep band of silver beading that encrusts the neck and hemline. Where would you find something of this quality today? Then there's this oyster pink backless evening gown, from the mid-1930s. I adore its heavy cowl neckline and its sweeping fishtail hem, not to mention the miraculous bias cutting which makes the satin drape like oil.

So yes, the superb quality of vintage clothing is a major part of this job's appeal. But for me there's something else. Something philosophical, almost. Please don't laugh, but what I love most about these amazing old clothes is the thought that they contain someone's personal history. I find myself wondering about the women who wore them. I find myself speculating about their lives. I can never look at a garment – like this early 1940s green tweed suit here for example – without thinking about the woman who owned it. How old was she when she bought it? Was she married? Was she pretty? Did she work? Did she have children? As it has a British label I find myself wondering what happened to her during the war and whether or not she survived it. Then I look at this pair of embroidered evening slippers here, and I imagine the woman who owned these dainty shoes rising out of them and walking along in them, or dancing in them, or standing on tip-toe to kiss someone. I look at this little pillbox hat on its stand, and I lift its veil as I'm doing now, and I try to imagine the face beneath it. Because the thing about vintage clothing is that you're not just buying fabric and thread – you're buying a piece of someone's *past*.

This is something I've always given a bit of thought to, not least because at times, when handling the clothes, and especially when trying a garment on myself, I've felt a sudden tiny shiver run the length of my spine as though *my soul* has in some way *connected* for a *split second* with the soul of its former wearer. I know it sounds crazy, but this has happened to me several times now; and it's even led me to wonder whether the spirit of a garment's former owner can in any way influence the life of its present one. No doubt you'll find this notion fanciful – the idea that a ghost can lurk in a suit or a dress; but something has recently happened to me – something shocking – which has made me believe that it *can*.

But before I tell you the story – and even thinking about it makes me feel faint – I need you to know how I source the clothes.

I mainly buy them at auction, especially at smaller provincial auctions where the prices are lower than in London; I also buy them from private sellers – either from people who bring things into the shop or who I visit at home. I also get clothes from specialist dealers who sell garments from a particular era. But whatever their origin I always try to find out at least a bit about their background, not just for its own interest, but because if there *is* a story then I like to tell it to whoever buys the garment so that its narrative thread, as it were, can go on.

For example, I sold an Ossie Clark 'floating daisies' dress last week, and I knew that it had once belonged to Julie Christie because she had given it to a friend who had given it to her daughter who, thirty years later, sold it to me. The woman to whom *I* then sold it was thrilled to know this about the dress and said that it would very much add to the pleasure of wearing it.

But to return to my own story. Sorry, I just need

a moment to collect myself. I've been feeling very shaky lately. All right . . .

I often buy things from an American dealer, Rick, who specialises in US clothing from the 1950s. He goes to and from the States buying and selling Rockabilly gear, what I call 'Preppie Americana' menswear – sleeveless jumpers, Brooks Brothers blazers and sea island shirts. Rick also sells prom dresses, those wonderful jewel-coloured strapless evening dresses with satin bodices beneath which foam layers of stiffened tulle sparkling with sequins. These dresses are so ridiculously glamorous and frothy that I call them 'cupcake' dresses. I hang them on the wall, like paintings, because I simply love looking at them – they make me feel *happy*. As you can see I have three of them over there – that candy pink one, the lime green one and the cornflower blue with the lace banding. There was a fourth dress which was the most glorious, intense yellow you could imagine. I sold it a fortnight ago. But what I've learned since has so upset me that I doubt I'll ever buy another prom dress again.

When Rick showed me these four dresses at his small warehouse in Camden I asked him, as I always do, whether he knew anything about their background. He told me that he'd bought them from a young woman in L.A. who said that they'd belonged to her great-aunt and that they'd just been in a trunk for fifty-five years. Rick added that this girl had behaved rather strangely, as though there was more to say about the dresses but that she hadn't wanted to tell him.

Anyway, I was sitting in the shop one quiet Wednesday lunch time three weeks ago when a couple walked in. I immediately thought how odd they looked together because the girl was about twenty-five while her boyfriend was a good fifteen years older, maybe more. She was very pretty and petite – no more than five-foot-two, with glossy shoulder-length dark hair, warm brown eyes and an olive complexion – but with a noticeably hesitant, unconfident demeanour. The man was big and broad-shouldered with hands like paws. While she looked through the clothes he sat on the white sofa, which he almost filled, thumbing his Blackberry. The girl spent two or three minutes going through the evening wear rail, apparently finding nothing. Then she looked at the cupcakes and I saw a light come into her eyes.

'How much is that yellow dress?' she asked me quietly.

'It's £300.' She nodded slowly. 'It's 100 per cent silk,' I explained, 'with hand-sewn crystals. Would you like to try it on?'

'Well...' The girl glanced anxiously at her boyfriend. 'Is that okay, Clive?' He looked up from his Blackberry and the girl indicated the yellow prom dress which I was now taking off the wall.

'No, it's not okay,' he said flatly.

The girl's face fell. 'Why not? It looks about the right size.'

He continued thumbing his Blackberry. 'It's too colourful.'

'I *like* bright colours.'

'It's not appropriate for the occasion.'

'But it's a dance.'

'It's too colourful,' he insisted. 'It won't do. Plus it's not nearly smart enough.' At that my dislike of the man turned to detestation.

'*Let* me try it,' the girl pleaded. 'Go on.'

The man looked at her, rolled his eyes then turned back to his Blackberry. 'Ok-ay,' he sighed. '*If* you must.'

I showed the girl into the changing room and drew the linen curtain round the rail. When she emerged a minute later I drew in my breath. The dress fitted her perfectly and showed off her tiny waist, lovely shoulders and slim arms. The deep yellow complemented her dark hair and warm skin while the subtle corseting flattered her bust. The tulle petticoats billowed around her in soft layers, the crystals winking in the sunlight.

'You look gorgeous,' I murmured. 'Just . . . *lovely*.'
She looked at me in the mirror and smiled, and as

she did so she reminded me suddenly of a canary –
a beautiful canary. 'Would you like to try on a pair
of shoes with it?' I asked her. 'Just to see how it
would look with heels?'

'Oh I won't need to,' she said as she stared at
herself, on tip-toe, in a side mirror. 'It's just . . .
fantastic.' She seemed overwhelmed, as though she'd
just been told some wonderful secret about herself.
She gazed into the mirror again, turning this way and
that, and now I suddenly noticed that her eyes were
shining with emotion. 'It makes me feel like I'm in .
. .' She swallowed. 'A fairytale.' She glanced nervously
at her boyfriend. 'Isn't this dress gorgeous, Clive?' He
didn't reply. 'Isn't it just . . . to *die* for?'

Clive looked at her now, then shook his head and
returned to his Blackberry. 'Like I say,' he said. 'Much
too bright. Plus it makes you look like you're going
to hop about in the ballet, not go to a sophisticated
dinner dance at the Hilton. Here.' He stood up, went
over to the evening rail and pulled out a Hardy
Amies black wool crepe cocktail dress and held it
against her. 'Try this.'

'But I don't – '

'*Try* this,' he repeated.

Crestfallen, the girl retreated into the fitting
room, emerging a minute later in the Hardy Amies.
The style was far too old for her and the colour
drained the warmth from her complexion. She

looked as though she were going to a funeral.

'*That's* more like it.' Clive looked at her with evident satisfaction. Then he made a circulating gesture with his index finger and the girl rotated for him, wearily, her eyes turned to the ceiling. I saw her lower lip quiver.

'Perfect.' Clive thrust his hand into his jacket. 'How much?' I glanced at the girl whose chin was dimpling with distress. 'How much?' the man repeated as he flipped open his bulging wallet.

'But it's the yellow one I like,' she croaked. 'I like the *yellow* one.'

'Then you'll just have to buy it yourself, won't you? If you can afford it,' he added pleasantly. He looked at me. 'I'll ask you again,' he said evenly. 'How *much?*'

'Oh. £150,' I replied, wishing that I could charge him three times that amount and give the girl the cupcake dress.

'Oh Clive. *Please*. I love that yellow dress, I just . . . *adore* it. It makes me feel . . . I don't know . . .' A tear fell onto her cheek. '*Happy*.'

'C'mon, sweetheart,' he moaned. 'That little black number's just the ticket and I'm going to have some important clients there so I don't want you looking like bloody Tinker Bell do I?' He glanced at his Rolex. 'Now stop messing about – I've got a conference call with the architects about the

Kilburn development at three. Now – am I buying this little black number or not? Because if I'm not then you won't be coming to the Hilton with me on Saturday, I can tell you.'

The girl hesitated for a few seconds then nodded mutely.

As I tore the receipt off the electronic reader the man held his hand out for the bag then slotted his card back into his wallet.

'Thanks,' he said briskly. Then, with the girl trailing disconsolately behind him, he left.

'So much for her fairytale,' I muttered as the door closed behind them. I felt almost as heartbroken as she did, not least because when a dress I love suits a customer so beautifully then I desperately want them to have it. I felt sad too that such a pretty young girl had opted to be with such a domineering older man. I presumed that it must be his money which attracted her to him, not that I was in any position to judge. God knows *I'd* gone out with some pretty awful men when I was her age. Nevertheless I found myself longing for some gorgeous Prince Charming, no more than thirty years old, to sweep her out of Clive's clutches then charge down to the shop with her and buy her the dress.

So potent was this fantasy that I actually put the dress to one side with a 'reserved' label on it, hoping that the girl would come back. After two days I realised that I was being as irrational as I was being un-businesslike. Clive was clearly not the kind of man to change his mind. The girl would not be returning.

So it came as a very great surprise, the following Monday morning, to look up from a small repair I was doing to a Nina Ricci shirt and see the girl pushing on the door.

As she entered the shop she looked different, somehow, from how she had looked on the previous Wednesday. Her head was held higher, and there was a determined set to her mouth. And when she tried the dress on once more, emitting an audible sigh almost of ecstasy as she did so, she reminded me not so much of a canary, as of a sunflower. Without Clive's over-bearing presence she seemed transformed. And when she opened her bag and took out six fifty-pound notes and laid them on the counter she had an almost triumphant gleam in her eye.

'I'm so glad you've come back for it,' I said, remembering her disappointment – and my own – five days earlier. I carefully folded the dress into its paper carrier. 'I can't imagine anyone looking more wonderful in it than you will.'

The girl smiled at me. 'Thanks. But I simply had to have it,' she added, as though she felt she had to explain herself. 'Once I'd tried it on, I had no choice. You see . . .' She shrugged. 'The dress . . . *claimed* me.'

'Well . . .' I smiled back at her. 'I wish you lots of fun and happiness in it.' Hopefully without the horrible Clive I added mentally.

Of course I wondered afterwards what had enabled the girl to buy the dress when she clearly hadn't had the money for it before. Perhaps she'd sold a piece of jewellery, I speculated. Perhaps she'd asked her parents or a friend to lend it to her. Perhaps Clive had relented – an idea I instantly discounted. But however the girl had come by the cash, that was one of the happiest sales I'd ever made.

Or so I thought.

Two days after the girl bought the dress, and exactly one week after she first came into the shop, our weekly free-sheet, the *Hampstead Echo*, dropped through the letterbox. I put down my mending and picked it up. On the front page was the usual stuff about over-zealous traffic wardens giving tickets to school run mums. Then I turned the page and my heart stopped. There, covering the top half of page 2 was a photo of Clive. The piece was captioned 'Death of Local Businessman'. My heart pounding like a drum, I read on.

'Tributes have been pouring in to local property developer, Clive Simms, 41, who died in an accident at his home in the early hours of Sunday. Mr Simms, who had just attended a function at the Hilton, where he had allegedly been drinking, fell thirty feet from the balcony of his house on Fitzjohn's Avenue. His girlfriend of two years, Susannah Wiley, who found his body the following morning, is said to be distraught.'

I lowered the paper. My breath was coming in little gasps. And I was just trying to remember the exact demeanour of Susannah, as I now knew she was called, when she came in to buy the dress just – what? – *two days* after this had happened, when the phone rang.

I took a deep breath then picked up.

'Hi Sarah,' said Rick in his American drawl. 'I'm just calling because you know you asked me about the prom dresses you bought from me last month? Well I've now found out a bit about the background there.'

'Oh yes?' I said faintly.

'Well . . . to be honest I'm not sure you'd want to pass this on to anyone you sold them to because it seems they have quite a tragic story.'

'Really?' I felt my palm moisten as I gripped the handset.

'I was in L.A. again last week, and by chance I bumped into the girl who sold me those dresses. We were both in the Beverly Center doing some shopping, and she's pretty cute actually so I asked her for a soda. And as we were sitting there I suddenly remembered that you'd wanted to know some more about the dresses, so I asked her, and this time she said that she'd tell me their history. But I'm afraid it's none too nice.'

I stared out of the window. 'Tell me.'

'Well, as I said to you before, they belonged to this girl's great-aunt. She was a cocktail waitress in a bar in downtown Chicago in the early fifties. She was in her twenties and used to wear them for work. Anyway – I'm not sure you'd want to tell anyone this, 'specially anyone who buys the yellow dress.'

'Tell them what?' I asked weakly.

'Well, it seems the woman killed her boyfriend. Went round to his apartment in the dead of night and shot him.' I felt the hairs on my neck raise themselves up. 'She tried to make it look like a break-in, but a neighbour spotted her leaving. Apparently the yellow of her dress was so bright that it could be seen in the dark. Anyway, the poor kid went to the chair. She was only twenty-four.'

The floor came up to greet me. I sank onto my chair, the handset adrift in my lap.

'Apparently the guy was quite a bit older,' I could just hear Rick say. 'He'd bullied her for years so I guess something inside of her must have just, snapped.'

I lifted my eyes to the other cupcake dresses then blinked.

'*Sarah?*' I heard. 'You still there?'

The Common
Enemy
Natasha Cooper

Natasha Cooper was born in London and has always lived there. She was an award-winning editor for some years before leaving publishing to write her first novel. After six historicals published under another name, she found her natural home in crime, first with the lighthearted Willow King series, then with the Trish Maguire novels. She chaired the Crime Writers' Association in 1999/2000. When not writing novels, she reviews for various newspapers and journals, and does some broadcasting and occasional journalism.

The screaming started early that night, only a few minutes after *News at Ten* had started, instead of nearer midnight. Sue Chalmers swore.

'Don't let it get to you,' Dan said, chucking the *Evening Standard* on the floor by his chair. 'Block it out.'

'How can I? Night after bloody night. They have to yell like that to make it sound as if they're having fun, when they're really feeling sick as dogs from all the booze and just as unsure and lonely and wondering why they don't enjoy the stuff everyone else does as we were when we were in our teens. I'd like to ram their stupid little heads against the nearest wall and bash some sense into them.'

Dan pulled his long body out of his chair, brushing his hand casually against her hair as he passed on his way out. She was so tense the pressure on her scalp seemed like an assault instead of the comfort she knew it was supposed to be.

'I know,' she said through her teeth. 'They're only

young. And you hate it when I'm so vehement. But it gets to me.'

'Tea?'

'Why not?' She leaned back and turned her head so she could smile over the back of the chair. 'Sorry.'

The newsreader was talking about the Middle East and Sue hated herself for getting so wound up about a bit of irritating noise when there were people out there living in hell. Dying, too. A dose of that kind of reality would sort out the shrieking, drunken teenagers and make them see what really mattered.

When silence fell five minutes later, it was like warmed oil oozing into an aching ear. Sue felt able to concentrate on the news again. Dan came back with the tea. This time, his hand on her head felt right, kind. She leaned closer to him.

Ten minutes after that footsteps sounded on the narrow pavement outside. They were even more familiar than the partying teenagers' screeches: Maggie Tulloch from three houses down was on her way home from another long stint in the probation office. Tonight her feet were dragging more than usual. She must have had a frustrating day. Sue liked her, and admired the way she went on and on trying to make her clients behave like human beings instead of filthy, thieving thugs.

* * *

Maggie heard Sue's television as she walked past the windows of number 23, knowing she had only a minute-and-a-half more of freedom. You shouldn't use your job as an excuse to stay out late, she thought, then took some reassurance from the knowledge that her work mattered.

If only one of the miserable, infuriating, self-indulgent, drug-addled ex-cons she had to deal with refrained from hurting someone else because of her efforts, then her addiction to work would be justified. The trouble was, none of them had refrained yet, and she'd been doing the job for thirteen years.

She stopped on her own front doorstep and had to force herself to get out her key and stuff it in the keyhole. The television was on in her house too, but unlikely to be showing anything as real or useful as the news. Leaning sideways to listen, she caught Celia Johnson's clipped and tragic voice, saying: 'It can't last. This misery can't last.'

Oh can't it? Maggie crunched her key in the lock and turned it.

'Hi, Mum!' she said aloud as she dumped her briefcase by the cold radiator and swung off her thin linen jacket to hang it over the end of the bannisters.

'You're late, darling.'

I wish you wouldn't call me darling, she thought, when everything else you say shows how much you hate me.

'Your supper's probably ruined, although I did turn the oven down a couple of hours ago. It's chicken.'

'No worries.' Maggie walked towards the kitchen, repeating Celia Johnson's thought: it can't last; this misery can't last.

How sensible it had seemed when her father had died only months after her husband had decided that married life and a toddler were not for him after all. She'd needed help; her mother, pension-less, work-less and utterly lost, had needed somewhere to live and something to do. Thirteen years ago.

The toddler was now fifteen, nearly sixteen. And Maggie's mother was not lost or uncertain any longer. Absolutely certain, in fact, about everything that was wrong with her daughter and the way she was bringing up Gemma, and not at all surprised Michael had decided to leave because who could possibly want to spend his life with someone who wouldn't eat what she was given, who dressed so badly, who swore so much, who was so work-obsessed she was the most boring person on earth, who was so ...

Don't do it, Maggie said to herself. Don't let her get to you. These are old battles and they can only be fought by two people. Refuse to fight back and she'll stop. One day she'll stop.

She listened again, then felt her neck muscles relaxing. For once there wasn't any thudding angry music from Gemma's room, distracting her from the work she had to do if she was to get anywhere near a decent university. Maggie looked at the kitchen clock. Ten-fifteen. That meant fifteen minutes to eat whatever was edible from the oven and calm down, then nip up to talk to Gemma and make sure she was feeling o.k. about tomorrow's exam, then a long hot bath and bed.

An open bottle of Australian shiraz stood by the cooker. She slopped some into a huge old rummer. It had been one of the few wedding presents Michael hadn't taken with him. Then she took herself to task, found a second rummer, polished it carefully, filled it with wine and carried both through to the sitting room.

'Oh, darling, is that for me?' Her mother glanced away from the screen for a second. 'Isn't it rather a lot?'

'You don't need to drink it all if it's too much,' Maggie said, lowering herself on to the sofa and letting her eyes close for a second. She took a deep swallow. 'Mmm. My drug of choice!'

'Don't be like that, darling. You're nowhere near addicted, even if you do drink ra-ather more than you should.'

'Thanks, Mum.' Maggie looked at Celia Johnson

being intensely unhappy on the screen and wondered whether the choice of film was meant as a reproach. She knew her mother was lonely, and maybe it wasn't her fault that she wouldn't even try to make friends or find herself any kind of occupation except watching DVDs of old films. 'How was your day?'

'Tiresome.' She flashed a long-suffering smile at Maggie, who smiled back and felt her jaw muscles crack. 'You know the gas man was supposed to deal with the boiler.'

'I remember. Didn't he come?'

'Of course not, and then there weren't any pomegranates left in the supermarket, so I couldn't do Gemma's favourite dish, which I'd promised her as a pre-exam celebration.'

'She'll understand.' Maggie drank again. 'And you've obviously managed her brilliantly tonight, getting her to work without that awful music taking half her attention away from her books.'

'Oh, she's not in tonight, darling. She needed a treat to relax her before tomorrow, so I gave her a little something to augment your mingy allowance and said she could go and see that friend of hers, who lives so near. Gillie, isn't it?'

Maggie put down her glass as though she didn't trust herself not to throw its contents all over her mother.

'You did what? On the night before an exam? Mum, how could you? You know how hard it's been to make Gemma take her work seriously. For God's sake!'

And then her mother laughed, with a pitying, condescending kind of amusement that turned all kinds of ancient levers in Maggie's brain.

'Funny how things change, darling. I can see you now, standing with your arms akimbo, thirty years ago, explaining to me precisely why I was the cruellest woman in the world when I forbade you to see your best friend on a school night.'

Maggie turned on her heel and headed for the kitchen. Even dried-out charred chicken would help stifle all the words she couldn't say, mustn't say.

I'm not a cruel woman, she told herself. Anyone would find this hard. It can't last.

She switched off the oven, opened the door and looked at the blackened stumpy chicken legs. There were four, which meant Gemma hadn't eaten before she left. The ration was always one drumstick and one thigh each. Her teeth were more than sharp enough to rip the hardened flesh from the bones of two of the joints, then she ran the cold tap until the water was icy, washing first her hands and then her face.

When she went back to the sitting room, she was calm enough to say: 'I know I was a tiresome adolescent, but you can't hold it against me for ever.

You know why I want Gemma to stay here on school nights. Encouraging her to rebel may give you satisfaction, but it's damaging all her chances.'

'Don't make such a fuss, darling. She'll be back any minute now. She promised to leave Gillie's by ten.'

'*What*?' Maggie reached for the phone, feeling the ground lurch beneath her feet. She knew the number as well as she knew her own, but for a few awful seconds she couldn't make her fingers work. At last she heard the ringing, on and on, then the voicemail cut in:

'Hi, it's Gemma,' came the light cheery voice. 'I'm having much too good a time to answer, so leave a message and I'll ring you back. Bye.'

'Gemma, it's Mum. Phone me.' It was at least three years since Gemma had last addressed her as Mum, but she wasn't going to call herself Maggie to her own daughter.

She found the number of Gillie's house and rang it. Diana, Gillie's mother, answered almost at once.

'It's Maggie,' she said, without any kind of greeting. 'Is Gemma there? I need to talk to her.'

'Oh, hi, Mags. No, she isn't. She left, what? Must be at least twenty minutes ago. She'd promised your mother she'd be home by ten. Isn't she back yet?'

'No.' The floor wasn't moving any more, but waves of heat and cold were washing through Maggie and she felt more unsafe than ever. 'It shouldn't have taken her more than six minutes at the very most. Did she leave on her own?'

'Of course, not. I wouldn't have let her. Jed was with her. You know, Jed Springthorpe, the most responsible boy in the whole school. She'll be all right with him. Honestly, Maggie. Don't fret. They've probably just stopped off for an illicit drink. Or a fag or two. I know they're not supposed to smoke, but I bet they do.'

Maggie muttered something vaguely polite, then cut the connection to phone Gemma's mobile again. Again she got the jaunty message.

'I'm going to look for her.'

'I'll come with you.'

'Mum, don't be silly. With your knees, I'll be quicker on my own. And someone needs to be here in case she gets back.'

Maggie thought there was no point bothering with a jacket. The air was warm enough. Even the pavements still held some of the day's heat. Thank God it was light still. Somehow this would seem even worse in the dark. And Gemma was nearly sixteen. Lots of people started work at sixteen. In her day, people of that age were travelling the world on their own. Maybe they still were. This panic was absurd.

But she couldn't keep it down. Something had happened. Gemma never turned off her phone. And she never left it to ring so long the voicemail cut in.

She was far, far too keen to have any kind of contact with anyone.

She and Jed could have chosen any of four different routes from Gillie's house on the other side of the main road. The most direct would have taken them past the local supermarket, but there were no enticing attractions to make them to linger there. It shut early on Mondays, so they wouldn't even have been tempted to drop in to buy drink. But two of other streets had pubs, and the third an expensive wine bar. Normally that would have been out of their reach financially, but tonight they had the money Maggie's mother had handed over.

Maggie pushed open the door of the first pub to be assaulted by heavy, pounding music, and excited yelling conversations. She almost fainted with relief when she saw the bright blonde straight hair of a tall slim girl by the bar.

'Gemma!' she shouted across the shrieky crowd. 'Gemma!'

Three girls looked round. None of them was her daughter. The girl at the bar turned her head lazily, perhaps wondering at the unexpectedly adult voice, and revealed herself to be a total stranger.

Maggie was out again an instant later, running now towards the other pub. She had no more luck. Outside again, she sent Gemma a text:

'RUOK? Pls phone.'

Then she waited, leaning against the wall outside the pub, among a bunch of curious smokers, staring down at the small screen, begging for an answer. Nothing came. She phoned again. Again she heard the message.

'Jed,' she said aloud, trying to think of the quickest way of getting his number. Her mind wasn't working properly. Gillie, obviously. But she hadn't brought that number with her either.

She began to run again, heading for home by the most direct route, needing to get to her address book as fast as possible. Her useless feet caught in every loose paving stone, until she gave up and kicked off her shoes, bending down to scoop them under one arm. As she righted herself, she pressed the speed dial for Gemma's number, and ran on, her shoeless feet keeping a much better grip on the paving stones.

Her tights ripped in moments, but that didn't matter, and once her right foot hit something soft, disgusting. Even that didn't make her pause. She ran on until a stitch savaged her midriff and forced her to stop just at the entrance to the supermarket carpark.

She'd forgotten the disabling pain; it was so long since she'd moved faster than a brisk walk. Gasping, fighting to get past the spasm, hugging herself, she looked at the long low buildings of the supermarket and thought how odd they seemed with no lights on and no cars lined up in front. Rubbish was strewn all round the recycling bins and the lid of the paper and cardboard one was propped open.

A ringing sound forced itself into her mind, and she looked down at the little phone she was carrying, sticky now from the sweat on her hand. The sound wasn't coming from there; all she could hear as she held it was a faint buzz, but the rhythm of buzz and ring was the same.

When she put her finger on the off button the ringing stopped, along with the buzz. She pressed the speed dial button for Gemma's phone again and the ringing started up. The sound was coming from somewhere near the recycling bins.

'She dropped her phone,' Maggie said, holding her right hand over her heart, as though to hold down its leaping and banging. 'That's all that's happened. She's not answering because she lost her phone. She's probably safe home by now and they're laughing at my neuroses again.'

Miraculously the stitch had gone, and the breathlessness with it. She felt fit and well and marginally more sensible.

She followed the ringing sound as she searched for the phone. If she could restore it to Gemma, it might help their continuing war, show how she understood that endless phoning was important, and texting and friends and doing everything except revision.

Another sound punctuated the ringing. A tiny gasping voice. 'Mum. Mum. Mum. Mum. Please. Oh, please. Mum.'

Maggie felt as if something had gone wrong with time, as though it was stretching out towards eternity. Her thoughts were racing, but each step took aeons to achieve.

Each recycling-bin lid she lifted seemed to weigh several tons. That agonising voice went on and on and the phone kept ringing. She reached the glass recycling-bin and fought with the lid.

'Mum. Mum. Mum. Please come. Please. Mum.'

This was the one. The voice was louder here.

'Gemma, darling, I'm here. Don't worry. I'm here.'

The light was much dimmer now. It must have been nearly eleven. But Maggie could see down into the blackness of the bin, to where her daughter lying in a foetal curl.

Gemma's head was a mass of dark-red stickiness, the laboriously straightened, gleaming blonde hair matted now with blood. Light from the street lamps caught edges of broken glass and showed cuts all up and down the bent bare legs.

Maggie leaned down to touch her daughter's skin, but her arms were too short to reach deep enough into the bin. She punched 999 into her phone, all the time saying Gemma's name, pouring out words of reassurance that meant absolutely nothing, because there was no reassurance to be had here.

'Police,' she said into the phone when they answered. 'Police and ambulance.'

'What's your address?'

She told them where she was and what she'd found, not saying it was her own daughter.

A patrol car drew up only two minutes later, and two uniformed officers got out, putting on their caps as they strolled towards her. Maggie couldn't speak now, just gestured towards the bin and stood back to let them see.

'Christ!' said one, pulling at his phone.

'I've already asked for an ambulance,' Maggie said, surprised to find that her voice still worked. 'Thanks for coming so quickly.'

She couldn't understand why the two officers looked at each other in such a weird way.

'We'll hurry up the ambulance,' said the woman. 'Come and sit in the car and tell me how you found this girl.'

'What?' Maggie stared at the officer's pleasant pink ignorant face. 'What d'you mean, sit in the car? I'm not leaving her.'

* * *

Later, hours and hours later in the hospital, she was sitting down, waiting. She'd told the police everything she knew. She'd phoned her mother to report and spent what felt like hours reassuring her. No, no of course it wasn't your fault. Of course you were doing what you thought was right. It was generous of you to give her money.

And then she'd come back here to wait, sitting on the edge of the hard plastic chair, not even noticing it was cutting off the blood supply in her legs until the pins and needles started actively to hurt.

A white-coated girl, woman, was walking towards Maggie now. The stethoscope banged her chest lightly with every step. Her expression was serious. Maggie ground the nails of one hand into the palm of the other, and waited again.

'She hasn't been raped,' said the doctor. 'That's one thing.'

'And the rest? How bad is it?'

'All head injuries are serious. She's taken quite a kicking. I'd say there were at least two of them. Scans show she's been bleeding into the brain, but we don't yet know the full extent of any damage.'

'And the prognosis?'

The doctor's face froze into blank, stubborn politeness, and something inside Maggie – some last vestige of hope – died.

★ ★ ★

'Darling! Darling, wake up!'

Maggie opened her gummy eyes. Moving her neck was agony. She'd fallen asleep with her head at an atrocious angle against the wall.

'I've brought you some coffee. Come on. It's a new day. You need to be strong now.'

'Have they said anything?'

Her mother bit her lip. 'Not yet. I got here about an hour ago, and they said they wouldn't know anything for a while. But the police are coming. They're going to want to talk to you, and I thought you'd like a chance to have some coffee, and maybe a wash even.'

Maggie was picking hard crunchy grits out of the corners of her eyes. She took her fingers away and looked at her mother, whose own eyes were covered with a film of tears.

'Come on, Maggie, darling. There's a cloakroom at the end of the passage. Shall I take you?'

A tiny smile was all she could produce, but she could see it registering, which made it easier to speak without snapping.

'I can probably manage. But thank you, Mum.'

Her mother's hand encircled her wrist for a second, then let her go. 'I'll be here with the coffee,' she said. 'And I brought a sandwich too in case you're hungry, but it doesn't matter if you're not. You don't have to eat it.'

Tears were pouring down Maggie's face as she headed for the loos.

* * *

The police officer who was waiting beside her mother looked much more senior than the two who'd come last night. He was wearing a suit made of some thinnish grey material and a white shirt, with a dark-blue tie.

'Mrs Tulloch?' he said, shaking her hand. 'I'm very sorry about what's happened to your daughter. Do you feel up to talking?'

'If it'll help,' said Maggie.

Her throat felt as though someone had stuffed it with wire wool they'd then pulled slowly up and down all night. And all her joints were stiff and painful.

'Didn't anyone see anything?' she said. 'Or hear it? I know the supermarket shuts early on Mondays, but there are usually people in the streets at that time. And there are houses all round. You can't be kicked like that and make no noise. Someone must have heard something. The marks on her body make the doctors think there were two of them at it.'

Which means it wasn't Jed, she suddenly thought, with real gratitude. Jed. Why didn't I think of him before?

'Has anyone found the boy?' she said aloud.

'Boy?' said the inspector. 'What boy?'

And so she told him about Jed, who was supposed to have been so responsibly escorting Gemma home by ten o'clock.

'Have you got a phone number?'

'No. But I can get it for you.'

'Or a surname?'

Her brain had shut down again as guilt poured through it. What if Jed had been in one of the other bins, bleeding all night, bleeding out maybe? Dying? And she hadn't said anything.

'Gerald Springthorpe,' said her mother.

'Was he – I mean, *is* he Gemma's boyfriend?'

'No. Just a friend. They're all at school together, so he's probably sitting in the exam room now.'

Maggie noticed that her mother was talking absolutely normally, sensibly, without any carping or martyring herself. She was in charge, and in some weird way it helped.

'We'll talk to him later. Can you tell me . . .?'

His voice seemed to be coming from further and further away. Maggie's temperature control had gone again. Shivering, boiling, she felt the floor tilting upwards and then nothing.

They'd found Jed by the time Gemma was pronounced dead three hours later, and one of the DI's juniors was relaying his story to Maggie. Listening to it helped to hold her in the present, but it couldn't stop the tears that came out of her eyes in great gouts. More fluid than she'd ever have believed a body could hold. She didn't even try to stop them, or dry her face.

'He says they were together all the way to the Bull, then a mate of his called out and wanted them to come in for drink,' the police officer told her. 'He says Gemma refused, said her nan would kill her if she was late home again. He said o.k, he'd take her to the door, then come back to join his mate in the pub, but Gemma asked him if he thought she was a baby.'

'So he let her go,' Maggie said, thinking what tiny things had made this huge unalterable disaster: her own insistence on not being out late on school nights; Gemma's pride; Jed's friend hanging around the pub at just the wrong moment.

'It wasn't his fault, Mrs Tulloch. Really it wasn't.'

'Didn't he hear anything?' Maggie said. 'It was only a street way. She must have screamed.'

Then she thought about the noise she'd heard in the pub. Jed had probably been inside then. If she'd known, if he'd recognised her, would there have been time to find and save Gemma?

Maggie bent over her knees, fighting to keep the howl inside her body.

'With all that music no one could've heard anything from outside,' the officer said, then echoed her thoughts: 'You'd know that I expect. I mean, you were in there yourself. We've got you on the CCTV, calling her name. Jed and his mate were there, too. The film proves his story.'

'So no one knows who did it?'

'Not yet. I'm sorry, Mrs Tulloch. We're doing everything we can. We've taken every possible kind of sample. The labs will . . .'

Maggie stopped listening. What did it matter anyway? Gemma was dead. It could've been anyone – one of her own clients, even, hanging about, bored, grabbing a passing girl to rob her of her phone and whatever pathetic little amount of money she had.

Had she fought back? Was that why they'd kicked her to death? Or were they crack-crazed thugs, getting off on her terror and their power?

'What about the secret cameras by the bins?' said her mother.

Maggie raised her sodden face and saw the officer looking sceptical.

'What secret cameras?' he said.

'The council put them there by the bins only a few weeks ago. One or two of the sluttier neighbours were flytipping nearly every day. Dumping their smelly rubbish in the recycling bins. So we got the council to put the cameras there. They should've had film in and been running. They must show what happened.'

* * *

'It'll haunt me until I die,' Sue Chalmers said to Dan that night. 'They were only thin scraggy boys who did it. Twelve-year-olds. You and I could've fought them off, stopped them killing her, if we'd known. But how could we know?'

'It's not our fault. I phoned the cops when we heard the screaming but it took them more than half an hour to come.'

'You did what?'

'Like you, I thought it was just kids making a racket, enjoying themselves, so I rang the local nick to complain, instead of 999. By the time they got round to investigating, poor Maggie Tulloch had already found Gemma. But at least they've got the boys now, and the evidence to prove it was them. They'll definitely go down for it.'

'I don't suppose that'll help Maggie, though. D'you think I ought to go round and see her?'

'No. You'd be intruding on that awful grief. And she's got her mother with her, after all.'

Planting Trees

Virginia Ironside

Virginia Ironside is a writer and journalist, best known for her role as agony aunt at the *Independent* and columnist on the *Oldie*. She's published fifteen books, her latest being *No! I Do't Want to Join a Bookclub*, the humorous diary of a sixty-year-old grannie.

Even though I was now married – eventually I found a historian called Ben, whose good points outnumbered his flaws by a narrow squeak – even though I was married, as I say, I could still remember Sky in great detail. Sad, really, because I hadn't seen him for forty years.

Sky – a real tit-arsed name if you hear it now, in the twenty-first century, but back when I was young, in the sixties, Sky was an extraordinary name. I mean, it wasn't like today when every single parent bursting out of her trackie bottoms with a fag in her mouth calls her child China or Zog.

No, in those days it was an exceptional name. And Sky was, for me, then, an exceptional person.

Sometimes, when Ben was droning on about the First World War for the twentieth time – men are so sentimental about war – I would think about Sky and wonder what had happened if things had been different. 'It might have been' – the saddest words in the

English language they say. I'd lie in my bath, recollecting him in as much detail as an Atkinson Grimshaw painting.

He was, actually, ludicrously good-looking. He was tall and thin, the sort of man who could wear a bin bag and it would just hang well on him. Everything about him looked well designed. His fingers never hung in awkward positions, always in classical poses, and even his feet, when I first saw them, featured the aristocratic long second toe. As he hardly ever spoke I had no idea whether he was actually bright or not, but he had a brooding presence that made everyone in the room look at him, even if he was just squatting in a corner reading a paper. His hair curiously soft, rather like a poodle's coat, longish and curly, and his face was like the bust of Caesar Augustus. It wasn't just the chiselled features, the noble nose and slightly cruel mouth, but it was the impassivity as well. He could have been made of stone.

Very occasionally, he would smile – and all that would happen is that a tiny muscle on the side of his cheek moved slightly and his eyes would show, suddenly, a pale warmth. I used to live for that smile.

In fact, if I'm honest, I used to live for Sky.

We'd met when I was at art school and he was just drifting up and down the King's Road. That's what a lot of people used to do in those days. Just drift up and down the King's Road, up and down. They might occasionally sit, silent, in the Kenco Coffee House, over an espresso, raising an eyebrow about a millimetre when a friend came in, and perhaps mumbling a 'Hi, man' (pronounced 'hermn') but that was about it. Not that they had friends in the way I think of them now. Friends were tremendously uncool. In fact, any kind of enthusiasm at all was uncool. Many of them modelled themselves on a guy called Rimbaud, a French poet who died young, a kind of shabby druggy anarchist one of whose best-known works was entitled 'A Season in Hell'.

Like Rimbaud, the members of this King's Road crowd all came from upper middle-class families, had, fashionably, dropped out of university, and presumably lived on trust funds. They were friends of people with surnames like Guinness and Ormsby-Gore and they often got killed in car crashes or lost all their parents' money in gambling joints. Quite a few had been in prison for running off with heiresses' daughters when they were fifteen, and so on. They liked the company of young aristocrats like themselves, affecting the same Byronic poses, but they also liked burglars and gangsters. The Krays, they thought, were very hip. A golden youth determined to be doomed. They would have despised today's go-getting yuppies. Drink was acceptable, but mostly they smoked dope.

When, one day, Sky beckoned to me in the coffee house and pointed to a chair, I obeyed instantly. We sat in silence for about an hour, until he rose slowly to his feet, muttering 'Gotta split.' At the door, he drawled, 'Party. Tonight. Twenty-four Cambridge Road. See you.'

We continued like this for about three months. He still said very little. He hardly said anything even when we slept together – the first time, for me – and I don't think either he or I enjoyed it very much. It's difficult to enjoy sex when you're being cool all the time. You just have to get it out of the way, like a rather loathsome necessity. I never even saw where he lived – if, indeed, he lived anywhere at all. We were always bedding down in friends' flats, or in the houses in Cheyne Walk owned by parents who were off, say, to Nice for a month.

When I once asked him – it just popped out, this dreadful uncool question – what he wanted to do with his life, his answer was, after a thirty-second pause and a thousand-yard stare: 'Plant trees'.

Just those two words struck me as so romantic and meaningful, that I could hardly speak. I had no ambitions like that. I think when I was young I'd once found a chestnut and put pins in it so it would balance on the top of a jam jar of water, and it had sprouted (or was it an avocado?) but you wouldn't actually call that planting trees.

But sometimes he'd buy a copy of a comic, like *Beano* or *Topper*, and explain to me how the strips of Desperate Dan, or Dennis the Menace or Beryl the

Peril were, in fact, metaphors for an anarchistic society and I'd listen, as mesmerised as a little boy listening to stories told by sailors from faraway lands. One day he referred to me, in front of someone else, as 'my bird' and I felt as if I had scaled a pinnacle of happiness.

Sometimes, when we went to parties held in parents' houses, we stole small things. I remember one night at three in the morning, looking at the blackness of the Thames over the wall at Chelsea Embankment, and we got out our stash. There was a small miniature of a horse from the downstairs cloakroom, an invitation to a dinner at the Mansion House, an Edwardian silver dressing-table box, a card from the loo on which was written the words: 'Pull down Slowly and Release Gently.' After about three minutes, he pushed everything into the river. But he kept the card.

'It's cool,' he said, and put it into his pocket. It was at this point he gave the very tiniest of smiles. Then he got out a cigarette (he called them 'snouts') turned his back on me and walked away.

Once he seemed to be living in a cottage in Kent near the Isle of Sheppey. He seemed fascinated that the inhabitants of this island had a reputation for being in-bred. When he discovered one of them with three fingers, he asked her over and painted a picture of her hands. It wasn't very good but, he said, it 'was just a study for a bigger work.'

I stayed with him there, once. Or rather, I drove

down. He seemed to have filled the house with glamorous people. He mumbled that Mick Jagger was coming. But before I left I got an urgent phone call from him, asking me to pick up a package from a house near Lots Road. I'd knocked at the door, and before it was opened, a voice shouted: 'Who's there?' from the inside. When I told them I came from Sky, there was unlocking of bolts and a rather grubby middle-aged woman opened the door and thrust a small, yellowish parcel into my hands.

'You driving?' she said. I nodded. 'Put it in the boot,' she said. 'Safer, if you're stopped by the fuzz.'

It was only when I'd got onto what then was the A20 – the M20 had yet to be made – that I realised that probably what I'd got was drugs. I drove much more carefully after that. I gave the package to Sky, who just nodded, and after that it was clear I wasn't really welcome, so I pushed off home, crying my eyes out.

During those three months I was with him, I even got pregnant. Not quite sure how because he was hardly the most passionate of lovers. But I suppose passion has nothing to do with it. It was one of those weird things to do. Half totally mad and half rather sensible. Mad, because clearly there was no hope to it. Sensible, because it clarified the situation, even if the clarification didn't give me the result I wanted. The minute I told him, his face became more stone-like than ever. He gave the tiniest of shudders. 'Cool,' he said. 'But count me out.' So I had an abortion and spent an afternoon in a basement in Harley Street – I'd had to bring £200 in used notes – and then the rest of the week at home in bed, weeping. I didn't hear from him, but I'd got so used to this behaviour that it took me a long time to realise that he had, in fact, dropped me.

It's difficult to explain what happened to me after that. All I know is that I became obsessed with him. I dropped out of art school and walked up and down the King's Road myself, looking for him. No sign. I met a friend of his who said he'd gone to Morocco and was living in the souk in Marrakesh. Another said he was living with an Indian heiress and was shacked up with her in a palace in Delhi. Another said she thought he'd died of an overdose. Eventually I heard he had married for about five minutes (apparently immediately after the wedding he said to her: 'Gotta split. See you around.')

This obsession went on for six years. I just thought about Sky, day and night. One year I got a postcard from him from South America showing yards of scrub. 'If you're ever this way, drop in,' it read. 'Sky.' But, typically, he didn't put an address – or I would have gone, scrambling over the desert to get to his tent. Just to sit on the sand beside him would have been enough for me. When I was with him I felt safe. Protected. It was completely irrational because anyone less protective than Sky you couldn't imagine. But there was something about him that felt, to me, like home.

It got so bad eventually that I had to see a therapist. He was one of those bearded men who sat impassively in a swivel chair with his legs uncrossed, behind a low table on which was a spider plant, a box of Kleenex and a glass of water.

'Does he remind you of anyone?' he asked, once. He was, actually, almost as impassive as Sky, but in an incredibly unattractive, nerdish way. He rarely said anything, either, but that wasn't because he was cool, it was because he was an idiot.

'No,' I said.

'I was thinking, perhaps, of your mother.'

'Were you?' I asked, surprised. Why should my mother have crossed his mind, I wondered?

'Cold, unavailable. Do you associate love with unavailability?'

'Doesn't everyone?' I asked.

'Perhaps your father?'

'No, not a bit like my father,' I said.

But of course he had a point. Aren't we all longing, in love, to get back to being a baby, to being nurtured, to being cared for? And if your parents are distant, then surely you go for distant men.

Eventually I dropped out of therapy and met Ben. Not ideal, and, as I say, he buried himself in his work too often, but, when he wrenched himself away from the past, he was a friendly sort of sexy companion.

'He'll do,' I said to myself, rather unkindly. And I remembered Rupert Brooke's poem.

'And I shall find some girl perhaps, and a better one than you,

With eyes as wise but kindlier and lips as soft, but true,

And I daresay she will do.'

Mean, I was.

But I never forgot about Sky.

I often wondered how he was now, but I hadn't heard from him for years. His presence was like the very faint drone from a radio that you'd turned down to nought, but which you hadn't actually turned off. I did hear from someone who'd seen him at a party and he said he'd mentioned my name to Sky, but apparently he had looked mystified. Or maybe he hadn't heard. I knew his father had died, so presumably he came into some money, I knew he'd been painting, and I always wanted to see him again. To lay a ghost to rest. To have a proper talk with him now he was older, and find out what exactly had happened when we were together.

I'd changed, heaven knows. I'd had two children and a successful job. I'd learned a bit about enthusiasm and how it wasn't as frightening as it used to seem. Children, with their hands all over you and their slobbering kisses and their crying and their tiny hands seeking for comfort in yours – they break the glamour of the 'cool' myth pretty swiftly. Ben was just distant enough, in an academic kind of way – historians always find it hard to get into the present – and yet loyal and loving and kind. I mean, he remembered my birthday and things like that. Very nice. I liked his parents, too.

Then one evening, not long ago, near Christmas, Ben was asked to one of those Chelsea street parties and wanted to meet me there before we went out to dinner. I say street party – I don't mean like the Silver Jubilee thing with trestle tables and sausage rolls and bunting, but rather a kind of open day for posh antique shops. You roll down around six-ish and you can wander into any shop you like and pick up a glass of wine and a canapé and stare at Victorian samplers costing hundreds of pounds (wishing all the while that you'd bought more of them when you could have got them for 6d in the 'sixties) and then you wander down the street and pop into another one and repeat the whole process. There's a smell of punch and cinnamon and the idea is that you mop up a few Christmas presents there – a marble bust for your wife's London garden, a necklace for your daughter, a retro thirties fountain pen for your son in the city. All done and dusted for about ten thousand quid. It's a kind of upmarket bar crawl. And the whole street is lined with Rolls Royces with chauffeurs sitting on the bonnets having cigarettes, and wandering around are any number of fat cats with broad pin-stripe suits and silk handkerchiefs sprouting from their top pockets looking smug.

As I plunged into the Chanel-heavy crowd of women with their throats stretched high, I searched for Ben. Instead, in among the throng, I saw a tall, but bent, figure, with a full head of white hair, and I was absolutely certain it was Sky. I say certain. Of course I wasn't certain. But it was quite easy to elbow my way through the guests, and view him from a distance. Like a wild animal, I became braver only slowly, but eventually managed to get up quite close and have a good stare. I couldn't hear his voice, but surely, I thought, that must be him.

His clothes – odd. He was wearing a rather grungy tee-shirt with a small self-conscious tear in it, over a pair of jeans. The tee-shirt had, once, been extremely expensive. He was, it was clear, trying to look young. Even though by now he must have been over sixty, he had a small earring and a faint stubble. Never a great shaver, his stubble was rather mangy. But he still had the same easy pose and the same low chuckle that I'd always found so irresistible.

I was overcome with a fit of panic. What would I say to him? 'Oh, hi there! Do you remember me? You took my virginity when I was eighteen, then you got me pregnant and then you dropped me and then I had a breakdown and here I am. Happy Christmas.'

I saw him looking at his watch. Then he made a

gesture to his companion as if to say: 'It's okay, I've got a few more minutes.'

With the panic of the same wild animal, I found myself aware that I had got too close and I darted out of the crowd. Why bother to say hello? What was the point? There was nothing to be gained. I wasn't going to rush off with him and have an affair. I was horrified to find that I was actually sweating, and suddenly terribly conscious of how very dowdy I looked. I had only dressed up a little bit – I was just meeting Ben, after all. I'd got on my flat comfortable shoes with the white scuffy bit at the toes, and my cardigan had been washed so often it was all down in the front and up at the back. My hair was in a mess.

But a part of me also said: surely I couldn't turn down this chance? Curiosity mingled with a faint sense of rather despicable yearning rushed into me. I started talking to myself as I would to my children when they sought my advice, and asked myself not only the question: 'How would you feel if you *did* go up to him?' but also: 'How would you feel if you *didn't*?' Anyway, he was going . . . he had a date somewhere. I wouldn't have to talk to him for long. What the hell.

I returned to the party, shuffled my way towards him and eventually stood, feeling rather like a dumb sheep, next to him, trying to make the two-person conversation he was conducting, into a triangle.

Eventually he turned, with the blank look of one who is rather irritated by the presence of a complete stranger. 'Why are you interrupting us?' his eyes seemed to be saying.

I blurted out my first name. 'And it is Sky, isn't it? I wasn't certain I recognised you ...' I said. Then, embarrassed, I added my surname, to help him retrieve me from his memory. He smiled, slowly. He seemed delighted to see me.

'Good to see you again,' he said. I imagined our entire past flashing before his eyes, but as in reality there wasn't a great deal of past to flash by – he wasn't to know I'd been pining for him for years – it didn't take him long. 'And what are you up to these days?'

Now this sentence was, I have to admit, for me, rather a blow. Very special people you've put on a pedestal don't say pedestrian things like 'And what are you up to these days?'

I gave the same textbook answer that was expected of me. 'This and that,' I said. 'And you? How are you keeping?' If he said 'bearing up', I thought, I'd have to leave.

'Bearing up,' he said.

'But how do you spend your days?' I asked, braver now. 'Why are you here? What keeps you busy?'

'Questions, questions!' He smiled. His skin, now he was older, was, oddly, rougher. God knows I knew that my bloom of youth had vanished several years ago, but his bloom had vanished, too. 'So what am I doing?' It turned out he was painting pictures, apparently, smoking a lot of dope, and living in a large chateau in France most of the time.

Then he said: 'I'm thinking . . . of planting some trees.'

Oddly, this statement didn't strike me as the words of Wonderman as they had when I'd first heard them forty years ago. I found myself asking myself why on earth he hadn't planted a few trees already. He'd had plenty of time to double dig, mulch, plant and water, I'd have thought. He could have planted forests by now. Suddenly my budding avocado seemed rather an achievement.

'And I've sent some slides of my pieces to Saatchi,' he added. 'I met him the other day.'

I blinked. The Mr Right of my dreams would never have referred to his paintings as 'pieces'. Nor would he have bragged about Saatchi.

'How strange to meet you again, and here of all places,' I said, burbling on, noticing, through the strategically-placed tear in the chest, of a couple of wiry white hairs.

'Don't you believe in the power of synchronicity, Virginia?' he asked, through hooded eyes, giving me a lowering smile.

I started at him. 'Power of synchronicity?' I said. 'No, I don't.' Then I added, somewhat sarcastically, 'Actually.'

'If ever you're in France, give me a bell,' he said. The only sign of his old self was the fact that he didn't give me an address or a phone number.

'I can't think of anything nicer,' I said, as we kissed goodbye.

But I could think of nicer things. Loads of nicer things. Meeting Ben, for one. I went outside and found him there, sipping a glass of wine.

'What are your plans?' I asked.

'Plans?' he said, rather puzzled. 'Well, I thought first of all we could escape this excruciatingly empty crowd, and then venture somewhere rather more civilised for supper.'

'Not plant trees?' I said, almost to myself.

'Plant trees, darling?' he said. 'Did you have too many glasses of wine? You big silly. Come on.' He steered me away. And as he did so, yesterday's fantasies fell away, dispersed into the evening traffic. I was aware of a huge sense of relief. And suddenly, I was hungry. Very hungry.

Remote Control

Polly Samson

Polly Samson's collection of stories *Lying in Bed*, and novel *Out of the Picture* are both published by Virago. She has written lyrics for Pink Floyd's album *The Division Bell* and David Gilmour's *On an Island*. She has also worked in publishing and as a journalist. Polly has donated her fee for her story to Childline.

'I wish we didn't have a television,' I said to Harry after a particular weekend of blaring cartoon, cheesy quiz show, soap and reality TV hell. All day Saturday while the rain hammered our forsaken garden Harry kept the TV loud enough to drown out the voices of our bored and bickering children. And yesterday, the sun tried its Sunday best to break through – at an annoying angle for the screen – so Harry drew the curtains.

'It's not what you watch that bothers me,' I said when he returned home this evening, delayed by yet another disorder on the Northern Line, and headed straight for his temple, dinner held before him like an offering to the Great God Prime Time. 'Its the time you waste doing it.'

'What are you?' said Harry, shooing Cato the cat who had been curled like a warm croissant in the comfy armchair that just happened to have the best view of the television. 'My mother?'

'Anyway, you watch it enough yourself,' he added, failing, as usual, to notice the little double flick that Cato gave with his tail before huffily stalking from the room.

How I wish I had a nice long tail like Cato's. Flick, flick, I'd go. 'Here's your dinner, Harry. Kept nice and warm for you,' flick, flick. That neat little gesture, as anyone who actually takes the time to talk to a cat will tell you, is the feline equivalent of the v-sign. Eff Off! Flick flick. Up yours! Flick flick What, dry food again? Flick flick.xf Stuff you!

Sighing in a way that only the sole breadwinner of a family can truly pull off, Harry lowered himself into his chair, dinner plate balanced on his knees. The television had been left on standby, its red light bright with the promise of pleasures to come. By the way he stared straight ahead at the screen I could tell that food was not uppermost in his mind.

'You're home too late to even see the children,' I said. 'Again,' I said.

Come to think of it I hadn't seen much of them since school myself and judging by the spewing video boxes on the floor, it looked like Amber and Archie had spent most of the afternoon in the company of the electronic faux-friend too. I knelt down to re-unite the boxes with the tapes.

'Perhaps you'd like me to make little home-movies of them in future?' I said, feeling my spite rise. 'That way you'll be able to recognise them should you ever need to pick them up from school.'

'That would be helpful,' Harry said, happily mashing extra butter into the plate of warmed-up mashed potato on his lap.

'Now, shush,' he said. 'It's time for *Stars and Their Drawers.*' Or something like that, how on earth am I supposed to remember the names of Harry's programmes? The room, I noticed, had a flat cola sort of stench to it and I wondered if Cato had been peeing in the fireplace again, because of the rain. Soggy paws have never been Cato's thing.

'Why don't you just sit down for once?' Harry sighed again, his hand scrabbling fruitlessly among the papers and sweet wrappers strewn on the table by his chair. He knocked a half-eaten honey sandwich to the floor, and then, because he didn't find what he was looking for, Harry lost it. 'Urrrmphhh,' he flung himself back into his chair.

'Where's the cruddy troll?' he hollered, paraphrasing Archie's imitation from five years ago of Harry in customary full TV-frenzy searching for the 'bloody control'. It had seemed quite funny at the time.

'Archie! Amber!' he bellowed through the ceiling, as though we had a brace of recalcitrant teenagers lolling around up there, and not two sleepy little children.

Sometimes I think he comes home in the evening just to madden us.

I found comfort with Cato in the kitchen. My lovely warm kitchen with its big family table and Archie and Amber's paintings on the walls and doors, Amber's half-drunk milk still on the table, the comforting purr of the fridge.

'What a hullabaloo,' said Cato, yawning pinkly. 'As for: "cruddy troll", don't you think it's time to lay off the tragic malapropism or what?' I could tell he was rather pleased with his own verbal dexterity; 'malapropism' being a word that not many cats use.

' "Who's *hidden* the cruddy troll," is the worst,' Cato added with a disdainful nod in the direction of the sitting room: 'So paranoid.'

Cato purred a little as I rubbed my biggest knuckle on the white hairs beneath his chin. Recently I've found that all my best conversations have been with Cato and this evening was no exception.

'Television will do for modern man what lead pipes did for the Romans, you mark my words,' he said as I scratched his little beard and felt my eyes well up. I would never dream of mentioning it to Cato but mortality being what it is there is an inherent sadness in friendship with a cat (or, I suppose, a dog too, if that's what you prefer). Wouldn't it be easier if it weren't seven of their years to one of ours? What will I do without him? Come to that, who will I talk to?

Cato snapped me out of my mawkish mood. He

arched his back, and bared his fangs in a tigerish fashion as the sound of the *Stars and Their Drawers* countdown came whooping through the wall. Harry had evidently located his holy grail without Archie or Amber's assistance.

'Even people staring at a blank wall have more brain activity than people watching television,' said Cato, calculating that Harry's viewing habits probably meant his cerebellum barely quivered in its fug of alpha waves. 'Harry's brain's about as active as a blancmange,' he said cattily.

It has always been soothing to find a true ally in the battlefield of the idiot box/electronic babysitter/mind-sucker/boob-tube/goggle-box. Call it what you like.

'Harry's "Plug-in drug" is what I call it,' said Cato as Archie shuffled into the kitchen, wearing his duvet as a cloak. Archie headed for the fridge, as though having been woken then shooed away by his father gave him special dispensation to eat after cleaning his teeth.

'Archie?'

Archie adopted his Oliver face at the fridge door. He's such a tiny boy for his age, it's often hard to refuse him food, though at that moment he was yawning.

'Dad woke me up,' he said. 'Can I have a chocolate mousse?'

I could hear Harry zapping through channels in the next room: studio audience laughter cut to a booming be-jingled assurance that 'nothing keeps a woman fresher,' and back to the same, or maybe a whole different, set of lemmings laughing.

'Dad said I could,' said Archie, sniffing.

At that moment, quite unbidden, a vision exploded before my eyes: a vision of my steak mallet smashing the TV screen to smithereens. It was so bright, this flash, that I almost shut the fridge door on Archie's fingers. 'To bed,' I hissed and Archie burst into tears.

'Fancy coming in this late, then waking the kids up,' said Cato as I was pouring milk of human kindness into the pan for Archie's hot chocolate following a penitent double dose of chocolate mousse.

'His father is perfectly capable of making hot chocolate, you know,' commented Cato sitting on the table, huffily pulling at his dew claws. 'Talk about remote control. I ask you!'

'Do you know,' I said deciding that I'd better divert Cato before he got too hissy, 'sometimes when Harry's watching TV, I play a little game. You should come in and watch.' I confessed to him how I occasionally amused myself by placing the remote control on the arm of my chair and then counted the seconds before Harry found an excuse to reclaim it.

'Uh-oh,' said Cato, in a rather drawly mid-Atlantic impersonation of Harry.

'Pass me the cruddy troll would you, darling? I think the colour balance needs adjusting.'

Cato stretched out on the table and looked me full in the eyes. 'It's the children I worry about,' he said, returning to his normal voice. 'All that television must take a terrible toll on their IQs.'

* * *

A child can get away with anything if it learns to look an adult straight in the eyes. Amber and Archie are both very good at looking me straight in the eyes. Not so Harry.

Harry hadn't managed to look at me once since our little fracas on Friday night when I informed him that I wanted to buy Cato something rather special for his birthday. In my defence, Cato has been saying that he misses having someone of his own species to chat to. He keeps mentioning some local Burmese kittens he's heard about. Apparently they are Lilac Burmese, a particularly attractive shade of pearly grey. (Cato says a Burmese would be best: there'd be a better chance of it turning out to be a Buddhist, like him.)

'I can't believe what I'm hearing,' Harry said, as the children ran in, wet from the garden and rowdy as kittens themselves. 'Are you seriously telling me,' said Harry, 'that you want to buy a kitten as a birthday present for the cat?'

'For Cato,' I said, realising as soon as the words left my lips that perhaps it did seem a tad unhinged. I felt a gust of cold air as the children opened the garden door. 'And let's not forget,' I added grateful for the Divine Intervention of sudden inspiration, 'it's Amber's sixth birthday in under a month.'

Harry clutched his jaw in both hands. 'Amber's having a bike,' he said. Amber, bless her, wrapped her arms around his knees. 'I want a kitten, I want a kitten,' she said.

'Yeah,' said Archie, hands on holsters and cowboy hat askew, 'and I'm having one too.'

After that Harry sulked for the rest of the weekend. He sat in that chair, and brandished the remote control like a spray repellent.

* * *

I almost fell asleep when I took Archie his hot chocolate. I lay upstairs in the children's dark bedroom, sharing a pillow with my little boy, his breath sweet as clover, with the comforting steadiness of my daughter's breathing coming from the next bed. If it hadn't been for the shrilling of television adverts through the floorboards it might have been one of those sublime moments of a life. My two healthy children and me, all breathing together like the sea. Instead, Archie started moaning that he'd never get to sleep with that racket, which woke Amber who had a tantrum when I told her to go straight back to sleep because I didn't really feel like making more hot chocolate, and below the television audience laughed and laughed.

Downstairs, suffering my usual capitulation at the sight of Amber's tears, I began heating milk for her chocolate. As I reached for the whisk from the brown ceramic pot of utensils beside the cooker, Cato jumped onto the work surface, and twined his tail around my arm.

'While you were upstairs,' he said in a stage whisper.

'Yes?'

'Well, you know how I hate to gossip,' he said. Cato can look quite kittenish when he's toying with something juicy. 'The thing is,' said Cato, rolling appealingly onto his side, 'I just overheard Harry on the phone, and he was ordering a Digi-box for the television.'

'Enough,' I cried. I grabbed the steak hammer from the brown pot.

'Eighty-five channels!' shrieked Cato as I swept from the room with the hammer in my hands.

Harry didn't see the steak hammer because he was kneeling on the floor, scouring the television page of the newspaper. Before I had even opened my mouth, Harry turned around and looked me firmly in the eyes. In his hands was the remote control and he was pointing it at me. The room didn't smell so bad anymore and I noticed he'd lit a real fire with some logs that he must've bought from the Greek shop on his way home. There was something touching about how he'd managed to light a fire without disrupting his viewing pleasure.

For the split second that the remote was aimed at me, I felt myself turn to ice. 'This is Harry,' I thought and shivered as I realised what was happening. 'And he's trying to switch me off.' Harry looked so handsome, and so warm, in his crumpled office trousers and rolled-up shirtsleeves, his wrists beautiful.

'Why won't you join me?' he said. 'I'm opening a nice bottle of cold white wine in the next break.'

'Ugh,' said Cato from the doorway. I've always loved Harry's wrists and at that moment he was placing the remote control in my hand, as though passing into my care something as delicate as a baby bird.

Harry rolled over to place another couple of logs on the fire.

'Sit down,' he said. 'It's about to be *The Big Blue*.

'Probably really embarrassing sex in it,' sniffed Cato.

'I'm sure you'll like it,' said Harry.

'I mean,' said Cato, 'here is a man who spends more time watching sexual content on TV than actually having intercourse.'

'Shush. How would you know a thing like that?' I aimed a friendly poke at Cato with my toe.

Harry looked genuinely hurt. 'Well, it's a guess,' he said. 'I should think I've known you long enough to know what films you like.'

Harry turned back to catch the exciting denouement of his favourite property show and I returned the steak hammer to the kitchen. Cato, meanwhile, manoeuvred himself between Harry and the set. He was all large eyes and drooping whiskers, doing his best imitation of a rescue cat – before it's been rescued. Or, perhaps I'd kicked him harder than I'd intended.

'I'm sorry,' I whispered to Cato.

'That's all right,' said Harry turning to face me. 'So, sit down, before it starts.'

Harry's smile can be quite dazzling in certain lights and firelight's the best.

'Don't fall for it. Remember it's the idiot box. It's the life-sucker.

'Come back to the kitchen,' said Cato twining in and out, around my legs. 'You don't need the plug-in drug, the tube for boobies.' Had he been trailing a rope rather than a tail he'd have been tying me with a figure of eight.

'Think of the radiation,' he hissed.

But already the screen was filling with a face even

more handsome than Harry's.

'Have I never explained about cultural imperialism and the western TV conglomerates?' Cato said as Harry squeezed my hand.

'Cato,' I replied sinking down into the sofa, my eyes filled with the sudden beauty. 'Why don't you go play with a mouse?'

Flick, flick.

Epilogue

Cato was run over not long after the installation of Harry's Digi-box. The new Lilac Burmese kittens, Beavis and Butthead, are now five, the age that Cato was when he died. Beavis and Butthead are indeed a very appealing shade of pearly grey but are a little in-bred and rarely have much of interest to say. They are largely ignored by Archie and Amber, who, though watching less television than their father – who has now up-graded the Digi-box to a Skybox with several hundred channels – have instead to be constantly shooed from the computer screen. Facebook is the new scourge and even Butthead paused from his eternal washing routine the other day to remark that it is partly financed by the CIA and Coca-Cola and that he can see no good coming of it at all.

The Karma of
Canine

Patricia Ferguson

Patricia Ferguson's last two novels, *It So Happens* and *Peripheral Vision*, were both published by Solidus Press and long-listed for the Orange Prize. Patricia lives in Bristol and teaches creative writing at the University there.

I'd put it down to grief, except I wasn't particularly grieving just then, I was sat reading the paper, with a cup of coffee, on a bright Sunday morning. Who'd conjure up a ghost in a set-up like that?

I think it's got something to do with my poor daughter Jilly, with what she's going through. It reminds me a lot of how I felt when she first moved out: that panicky helplessness. She was barely seventeen.

Oh, there'd been rows beforehand, years of rows, not only about the boyfriend. Darren.

I didn't care about his background, whatever Jilly said. After all, who was I to point any fingers?

'How can I be a snob?' I remember shouting at her. 'I'm just as much working class as him. If anyone's being prejudiced around here, it's not me, my girl!'

Darren: once he turned up on a Saturday at dinnertime, of course Carol tried to treat him like a human being, Oh come in, Darren, how are you, won't you join us, lots to go round, that sort of thing. But he hadn't a clue how to behave.

'No, I'm all right,' he said, and then he just stood there on the doormat with his hands in his pockets, not saying anything, just shifting from foot to foot and sighing like a windy horse, until Jilly got up; and then she didn't utter a word either, just clumped off with him in her great clod-hopping boots, slamming the door behind her as if she were leaving an empty house.

Aye, the delights of parenthood.

And she'd been such an easy baby, such a lovely little girl! Right up until secondary school. And then suddenly all her friends seemed to have parents who didn't give a toss what they did. She was out every evening, late as she pleased. Made no difference what we said. She was always threatening to run away: and then she did.

For a while I tried to hang onto my anger. She wasn't looking for a job, or trekking off to see the world, or doing something for charity; she'd just sloped off to live with her dolt of a Darren. And I'd say to myself, so be it. I felt like one of those characters in films who say, I have no daughter.

Then we went to the address she'd given us, and she'd only been there the one night. We had no idea where she was for four months. That was a grim time.

Anyway, the pair of them just walked in through the gate one Sunday afternoon in October. We were raking up leaves.

'Oh, Jilly, love!' Carol ran to meet them.

I had to look away: Jilly had this silver stud at the side of her nose. It's common enough now, but it turned my stomach then. But what made me drop the rake and go into the house to be alone was the dog. A half-grown puppy with a red spotted handkerchief tied round its neck.

In my book you got a dog when you were settled. It meant permanence. Permanent drifting in her case, committed shiftlessness.

After a bit I remembered my own dad's expression when I was nineteen and turned up one Christmas in tight blue velvet hipsters and shoulder-length hair.

I told myself: it's a dog, not a baby. And she looks like a beggar but she doesn't look ill. The stud will hardly leave a scar when she gets fed up with it, and she will. After all, had I kept the ringlets?

I had to grin at my reflection at that. Chance'd be a fine thing.

They were still in the garden when I came out.

'We're all going for a walk, are you coming?' says Carol, all brightly.

The puppy came wriggling up to me, wagging its ratty little tail. It was vaguely Alsatian-coloured, but with droopy ears. I've never liked dogs much, can't see the point of them.

'What's its name?' I said, and then I had a quick moment of terror, in case they'd called it after me, or my mother, something like that. Darren spoke. It was the first time I'd seen the lad smile, a sweet smile it was.

'She's called Zen,' he said proudly, and I burst out laughing, I couldn't help it. Calling a mongrel dog Zen, the dopey cheek of it! The Zen of doghood, the Karma of canine. I must admit: I rather liked it.

Anyway, off we went up Belbarrow, the highest point around here, and took it in turns to throw Zen sticks, she'd tear after them and sometimes pick them up, sometimes just carry on running, she was all over the place, circling and occasionally falling over in somersaults. She gave us all something to talk about.

'That's not going to last much longer,' said Carol when they'd gone.

'How d'you mean?' I asked.

'She's only seventeen. She can look after Darren, or she can look after the dog. I don't think she can do both. Do I sound heartless? Because my money's on the dog.'

Jilly came home for a few weekends after that. And at Christmas Darren and the dog came too. On the day, they cooked themselves a vegetarian nut roast like a welded heap of sawdust. Carol did us the smallest size of turkey, but there was still plenty of it.

'Would you like a little bite, Darren?' she asked him, and Jilly scolded, 'Oh, Mum!' before he had a chance to reply.

Late that night, when I was doing a last bit of tidying up in the kitchen, Darren came in to put the kettle on. I took a plate, twisted off the remaining turkey leg, and held it out to him. I meant to be kind; I'd seen him gazing at the turkey same as Carol had; but as I held the plate out I felt as if I were treating him like some wild animal, the way Carol puts out scraps at night for the fox at the bottom of the garden.

He took it without a word.

The dog was no end of trouble. Always barking her head off at anyone walking down the path, going mad at the postman, trying to kill next door's cat. She sat on the stairs, and chewed the banisters. We shut her in the kitchen, and she gnawed the table-legs and overturned the rubbish bin. She had no prejudices about only eating things that were actually edible; you could tell that from the messes she left all over the garden.

Not that either of them shirked clearing-up duties. The dog was what they were about, as a couple, Carol said. They certainly spent a lot of time stroking her and telling her what a beautiful dog she was, though she'd grown up pretty funny-looking, I thought, with slightly bandy back legs that made her bottom waggle as she walked.

Mind you, she was brilliant at catching a frisbee. Seemed to understand the idea of flight path. She'd leap right up like a gazelle as the frisbee came sailing down, and bite it very gently out of the air. Sometimes other people stopped to watch.

Then Darren went to Manchester to see his brother, Jilly said, but not looking at me, so I knew it was all up.

A little while later Jilly got accepted onto a foundation arts course. It was exactly what Carol and I had thought would suit her, we were thrilled. It was a struggle pretending to be only mildly pleased about it, though that seemed essential to Jilly's pride at the time. Again, Zen was a useful diversion. Jilly would have to board, but dogs weren't allowed on campus, so we could hide our delight in long wrangles about dog-care.

In the end, of course, we said yes. Just for the year. You take her back as soon as term ends, mind!

So there we were, stuck with the dog.

For a start she needed to go out, all weathers. I had to get up a whole hour earlier if I was to get her anything like tired before we went off to work all day. At first it was horrible getting out of bed. But after a while I began to enjoy the quiet and the dawn. I'd be up Belbarrow in time to watch the sunrise. Zen carried the frisbee, and wherever we went she was joyful, leaping into water, running uphill as lightly as she ran down.

When I got home she'd jump up at me whimpering with joy. It was a bit irritating at first, then I got used to it, the way I got used to being followed. She'd get up and accompany me to the toilet, or into the kitchen to put the kettle on. She wanted to keep me in view. I'd become the ruler of the universe, as far as Zen was concerned. It was disconcerting at first, to be so adored. Then I got used to it.

I could see why people have dogs, why some people need them. If you're uncertain inside, what could be more reassuring than a big ferocious animal treating you like the ruler of the universe?

At weekends we climbed all the peaks again. Sometimes Carol came, but long hikes aren't really her cup of tea. Zen and I went further and faster on our own.

Then I got my first mountain bike, and we went miles, any weather, any time, even at night! Sometimes at the weekend, especially if Carol was away visiting her mother, we'd be out all day, Zen and me.

One day, in the early summer, we went about thirty miles, ending up along the new bit of cycle path. About four, I stopped at a café and had a cup of tea, while the woman brought Zen a dish of water. When I went to leave Zen wouldn't budge. Just lay curled where she was, looking up at me.

'Come on, girl!' I said, but she didn't move. I nearly laughed; I'd tired her out at last! It had never happened before. I stroked her, and told her I was sorry, but we were going home now, we'd take it easy; and then I saw her paws.

All her feet were bleeding. I'd made her run, you see, on too much tarmac. Her pads were raw, skinned. She must have been in agony those last few miles, running along on her raw feet keeping up with me.

The worse thing was when I left her there. I'd explained things to the nice woman in the café that I'd got to go and get the car, and how soon I'd be back. But of course I couldn't explain it to Zen. She went berserk, she got herself to the door and tried to claw her way out of it, I could see her scrabbling scarlet pads through the glass as I unlocked my bike.

It took weeks for her feet to heal. She had these special dog-proof bandages and a thing like a bucket strapped to her collar, to stop her getting at them. I couldn't sleep at first, I felt so sick at myself for being so careless, and Carol suggested I bring Zen's bed up into our room, as a treat for Zen. It made me feel better too. That was the end of Zen sleeping in the kitchen.

By the time she was better I'd stopped even thinking of her as Jilly's dog. When Jilly came and asked us if we could keep Zen the rest of the summer, because she wanted to go off travelling, I couldn't think what she meant for a moment.

'She likes you best now anyway,' she said. She looked beautiful that day. I'd got used to the stud, I told her. She grinned, and showed me the tattoo on her upper arm. 'You know she'd choose you, Dad, if we could ask her. Wouldn't you, Zen?' Hearing her name the dog thumped her tail from beside my chair. That was always her favourite place. Her head on my foot, keeping me in view. It felt peaceful: the Karma of canine.

It was about a fortnight ago that I saw Darren in the street. I hadn't seen him for a good while, and he looked very different, better colour, not so skinny, and as we drew near he said 'Hallo', almost chirpily.

I stopped and asked him how he was, and felt for once that he wasn't struggling for the answer, but just replying:

'I'm grand. Got a baby now!'

'You've never!' I said.

'Three weeks old today. He's called Sean. He's grand.'

'Congratulations!' I said, wondering who the mother was.

'Is your Jilly wed, then?'

'Sort of,' I said. Living in London now, with her partner, Tim. I thought about telling Darren that she was going to have a baby too, but decided against it, in case it deflated him in some way.

Just a couple of weeks ago, that was.

My poor Jilly. There's no explanation for it. Everything fine one minute, and all over the next. Twenty-two weeks gestation, she was: a late miscarriage, they said. It would have been a boy.

That's where Carol is now. I had to get back. I felt a bit of a spare part after a while, to be honest. It's Carol Jilly needs.

I got home late yesterday, and as soon as I sat myself down after supper Zen came and squeezed herself in beside me, lay down and put her head on my foot.

Hallo, old girl, I thought, with such a rush of affection, and I reached down to stroke her; and then I remembered that she was dead.

I even looked. But of course there was nothing there.

It was a shock. Makes you doubt yourself. After a while I convinced myself that I'd simply imagined it, sort of half-remembered it. Because I do miss her, a lot. She's been dead over a year now.

There was a time when she'd started to walk after the frisbee, mind. And she'd turn round and set off for home when she'd had enough. She got to be an old lady, happy to stay in all day if it was too cold or wet. Her muzzle went white, she got a bit heavier, it was a real squeeze getting in beside my armchair every evening. But it was so familiar, her settling down movements, her sigh of contentment, her head on my foot.

Obviously I'd sat down half-expecting it. Imagination. And being so tired and so low, missing my wife, sorry for my daughter and Tim, missing the lovely hope and excitement we'd all had about the new baby. I try not to think about the actual lost little boy himself, that's too much.

But this morning. I'd just sat down with my coffee and the paper, and there it is again.

A slight shift of my chair as she squeezes herself in beside me; the little sigh; the delicate comforting touch.

Well, I'm not going to look this time. I'm not going to check. I'm just going to let her lie. As a sleeping dog should.

The Sound of
Snow

Nell Leyshon

Nell Leyshon is an award-winning playwright with work broadcast on Radio3 and Radio 4. She was brought up in Glastonbury and lives in Bournemouth. Her first novel, *Black Dirt*, was long-listed for the Orange Prize. Her second novel, *Devotion*, was published earlier this year by Picador.

The air was so cold it hurt Lori to breathe. She pulled the hood tight around her face and, keeping her hands driven deep into her pockets, walked as quickly as she could through the dark streets. She tried not to think of the warm bed she had just left, or the cool water she was about to enter.

The melted snow from her boots made pools of water on the cubicle floor as she shed her outer skin of padded coat and gloves. Then the next skin of fleece sweater and thick pants. Then her undershirt and underwear. Lori hated undressing. It seemed as though each time she looked at herself, she had changed. She just wished it was all over, so she could take a long hard look in the mirror and know exactly who she was.

She pulled on her tight nylon swimsuit and hauled it over each arm. It cut into her between the legs and on her shoulders: she had to get a new, larger one. She kept forgetting to tell her father, and wished he would just think of it. This was always how it was: nothing in their home was ever guessed. Nothing divined. Everything had to be stated crudely, out loud, however difficult. The usual thought began: if her mother was still alive . . . Lori stopped herself. There was no point thinking it. No point at all. She scraped her hair back off her face, tightly enough to hurt her scalp, and tied it. She removed her thick socks and her small pale feet touched the tiled floor.

There were long windows down one side of the pool and the snow was piled up against the glass, casting grey shade. The other girls were already warming up with the coach, practising their routine to the music: sailboats; verticals; ballet legs, and the frantic sculling which would control the submerged part of their bodies while surface composure was maintained.

Lori slipped into the water and took a few deep breaths. She sank down under the surface and pushed hard against the side. The artificial lights cast moving lines in the water, which rippled on the blue and white tiles. She easily reached the end of the pool and turned, pushed off. She felt fit, strong, and the second length began easily. Gliding deep down, her belly almost brushed the floor of the pool, then she rose slowly. It was then she realised she had a chance of being the first to complete the two lengths. She kicked, harder, stretched out as long as she could, drove herself forward. But as she let out some bubbles of air, she began to feel the lack of oxygen. She could see the wall ahead of her, but her lungs began to burn, as though they were being heated from beneath, and black spots appeared in front of her eyes.

She kicked again, and her lungs ached, and she felt so desperate that she was tempted to open her mouth. It would be like raising a dam and the water would rush in to fill her spongy lungs and it really wouldn't matter as nothing could be as bad as this feeling, where the spots grew larger and darker, and it hurt more than she could imagine. She finally touched the tiled wall and burst through the surface. The air rushed in through her mouth and she breathed heavily, her heart beating as a machine, her head resting on her arms on the side of the pool.

As soon as she left the building, Lori knew it had been a mistake to neglect to dry her hair. The wind had turned and even though she'd put up her hood, she could feel the clumps of hair turning to ice. Her nose ran and when she sniffed, her nostrils stuck together.

The air was fresh, smelling only of the cold, the air and the trees. She could hear the distinctive sound of the dry snow being compacted into the tread of her boots. It was something between a creak and a squeak, similar to the sound of the dentist filling a tooth, forcing material into the cavity.

She passed the small Town Hall and the store, both closed, then turned towards her house. It was white, and would be lost in the snow, if not for the green windows and doors, and the steady stream of smoke from the chimney. She walked up the drive and opened the small door on the side of the garage.

The smell of blood hit immediately. A caribou lay on the concrete floor, its head and torso skinned. Its raw, red flesh ended at the top of its fur-covered legs. The grey winter coat lay spread-eagled next to the animal, along with the severed antlers: large, male, scraps of flesh on the cut ends. Lori tried not to look but was drawn to the white fat, the clearly defined muscles. The bucket of blood and organs.

She forced herself to go through the next door, into the kitchen. She closed it quickly behind her and went into the hallway and, stopping only to rid herself of coat and boots, she ran upstairs to her room.

The hairdryer thawed and then dried her hair, leaving it full of static. Her skin was tight, and she put some cream on her face, and some petroleum jelly round her nostrils where she was sore and pinched.

She looked at herself carefully in the mirror: her thin face and pointed nose, her eyes red from the chlorine. She held her face with both hands, feeling the bone structure beneath. That's what counted apparently, bone structure, though it seemed to her that all bones were alike. One skull was much like another. One caribou head was much like another. It was the colour of the coat and the spread of antlers which seemed to differentiate one from another.

Her father sat with his socked feet up on the table. He filled the chair, nearly spilled out over the arms. Next to him their neighbour, David.

'Hello, Princess,' her father said.

Lori stood in the doorway. 'Why did you leave the caribou there?' she asked. 'You know I hate seeing them.'

'I knew you'd say something. Didn't I say, David? Didn't I?'

'You did.'

'Then why did you?' Lori asked.

'Don't be like that.' Her father turned to David. 'This is what happens. You have a little princess, then she gets older and she turns on you. Used to love coming shooting. Used to help me skin them and everything.'

Lori turned to leave the room.

'Where you going?' her father asked.

Lori sighed. 'To see Janine.'

'Talk some sense into her. That girl's driving me to an early death. Won't do anything I say. Won't listen, even.'

'That's girls for you,' David said.

'Yep,' her father said. 'That's girls.' He took his feet down from the table and called after Lori.

'We're leaving in twenty minutes, Princess. Make sure you're ready.'

Lori knocked on Janine's door, but there was no answer. She crossed the hall to the bathroom and knocked on that door. Again, no answer. She could hear some water running and tried the handle. The door opened.

Janine stood in the bathtub, a sponge in one hand, soaping her arms.

Her belly was rounded, and her belly button had protruded. She had a dark line running from belly button down to her pubic hair. Her breasts were larger than Lori had ever seen, and a different shape; the aureole were dark brown and her nipples swollen.

Janine looked up and saw Lori. She covered herself, one arm over her breasts, the other over her belly, and screamed at Lori. 'Get out. Get out.'

Lori ran, slamming the door behind her. She went straight into her bedroom and closed the door. She sat on the side of her bed for a while, then picked up her small globe and span it. Her hands still shook and the globe trembled.

The bedroom door opened and Janine entered. She was wrapped in a towel, her legs still wet. There was a tiny cut on her ankle where she had been shaving her legs, and a small trickle of blood mingled with the water.

She stared at Lori. 'You shouldn't have come in.'

'It wasn't locked,' Lori said. She lowered her head. 'I'm sorry.'

Janine shrugged. 'You're not to tell him.'

Lori stared, vacantly.

'He doesn't know. Okay?'

'Why not?'

'I haven't told him.'

'Are you going to have it?'

Janine nodded. 'I have to. It's too late to do anything.'

Lori put on her gloves and boots, and pulled a ski mask over her head. Her father was on the snowmobile, calling out for her to hurry and she ran and jumped on behind him. He started off immediately and they drove to the frozen lake.

Her father used the auger to cut a hole in the ice then assembled the line and threaded some fresh caribou meat onto the hook. He let the weighted bait down into the water and propped the line on the tripod.

Lori looked around. The frozen lake was a large white disc, fringed with deep green trees. There were no people: just the green and white, the crisp air, and her father jigging the line.

She thought of Janine back in the house, wrapping herself up, hiding her swollen belly. She turned and looked at her father, standing in silence, the snowmobile behind him, the lake stretched right out.

The sun was dropping down, brushing the tops of the trees. The sky was beginning to turn, each trace of cloud a different shade: grey, pink, yellow.

The day felt as though it was going on forever and she wished she could rewind and come back from the pool to find Janine in the kitchen making thick hot chocolate. Her father would be in the garage. He would look up from skinning the caribou (she wouldn't mind him doing it, as long as the bit about Janine could change), and ask how her training had been. She would tell him about the two lengths underwater, and he would pat her on the back. That's my girl, he'd say.

'Princess.'

Lori jumped and her father shook his head. 'You got to get to bed earlier. You need more sleep. Janine too.'

'Janine's sixteen,' Lori said.

Her father grunted. 'Sixteen's nothing. Still a child at sixteen.' He pulled on the line and she heard the tone of his voice change. 'Something here.'

Lori watched while he slowly and carefully drew the line in. The gaping mouth of a lake trout appeared. He eased it out of the hole and lay it down; the gills opened and closed, desperately searching for water.

He took the hook from its lip and hit the fish's head onto the ice until it was dead. There were traces of blood on the white. The still body, its dappled colours, like the late afternoon sky reflected. Her father dropped the line back in. They stayed there, silent for a long time.

'Dad,' Lori said. 'Would you ever want to move?'

Her father stared at her. 'Why would I want to do that?'

'I just wondered. Would you ever want to be with more people?'

He thought for a moment. 'Why'd I want more people? I got you and Janine. Got David and the other men around about.'

Lori nodded.

'Why d'you say that anyways?'

'Just wondered,' Lori said.

'You don't want to do that. You got your friends. Got the synchro team. Got your sister.'

'I know,' Lori said.

'Well then? Why d'you say it?'

'I spose I like to think about what it's like living in different places.'

'Ain't nothing to stop you doing that.' He punched her lightly on the shoulder. 'But look about you. Wouldn't get this no place else. Fresh air, all this space.' They both looked around at the white lake and the green trees, the sun dipping down now, its shape blurred by the tops of the trees. Lori thought of all the other fish in the water. Swimming under the ice, right under their feet.

'I know it's beautiful,' Lori said. 'But we're a long

way from anyone else. From anything.'

Her father shrugged. 'Got all we need here. Can't see the point of anything else. Got food, got heat.'

'But it's all flown in.'

'And?'

'If they stopped flying it in, what would happen to us?'

Her father laughed. 'We'd catch fish. Hunt. Cut down trees.'

'There wouldn't be enough to eat.'

'We'd survive. Anyway think of the summers. You wouldn't get a summer like here nowhere else.'

'And the blackflies?'

'Flies? Ain't nothing. Thing is, Lori, you don't know. You girls, you think you know things, but you don't know how safe you are here. Your childhood can go on longer here. None of that growing up before you have to.'

In bed that night, Lori held her small globe in her hands. She turned it slowly. There were so many places you could live.

The countries towards the North Pole were white, where the snow was laid over the land. She couldn't understand why she lived up here, where she had to dress up in all those layers, and her tears froze on her face.

The door opened and Janine came in. She wore her

nightdress with a thick fleece over it, and her blue bed socks. She sat on the bed and watched Lori turn the globe.

'What you doing?'

Lori looked up at her. 'You ever thought about why we live here?'

Janine shrugged. 'Always lived here.'

'But why?' Lori asked.

'Know what, Lori, you ask too many questions. It just is the way it is.'

Lori span the globe, her finger resting on it lightly. It slowed then finally stopped. She looked underneath her finger. Ethiopia. A land of sand and red skies, of heat and earth. She wondered if anyone in Ethiopia had a globe. Perhaps some girl one day had spun her globe in a dusty classroom and it had stopped, leaving her finger on Labrador. Perhaps she had wondered what it was like, and had conjured up a mind full of snow and ice and winds.

Janine stood up. 'Can I get in? It's cold in my room.'

Lori pulled the covers back and Janine got in. She reached over and turned off the light.

They lay in the dark silence for a while, then Janine turned onto her side. Her swollen belly pushed against Lori. Lori felt something move. 'What was that?' she whispered.

'It moves inside me,' Janine said. 'When I'm in bed.'

'What's it feel like?'

'Like I swallowed a live frog.'

Both girls laughed, then fell quiet again.

'How you gonna tell Dad?' Lori asked.

'I don't know.' Janine grabbed Lori's hand and placed it on her hard stomach. 'Feel.'

Lori felt a lump draw across the tight skin. She went to pull her hand away, but Janine kept hold of it. 'What's that?' she asked.

'It's just an arm or a leg,' Janine said.

They fell quiet again, then Lori whispered.

'I'll be an aunt.'

'You will.'

'Can I help look after it?'

'Course you can.'

They lay quietly for a while, then Lori said Janine's name.

'What?'

'You ever wish Dad had married again?'

'Sometimes,' Janine said.

'I do too.'

They lay there for a long time and Lori thought Janine must have fallen asleep. But as she felt her own eyes begin to close, Janine spoke.

'Lori. You still awake?'

'Yeh.'

Janine paused, then, 'Lori, I'm scared.'

Lori reached out and found Janine's hand and held it.

'Tell me I'll be all right, Lori.'

'You'll be all right,' Lori said. 'You will.'

Lori woke the next morning, stiff where she had been pushed right to the edge of the bed. Janine was breathing through her open mouth, her hair over her face. Lori crept out of the bottom of the bed and went down to the kitchen.

Her father was making breakfast, dressed in his thick snow pants and a shirt.

'Morning, Princess.'

Lori sat at the table and rubbed her eyes.

'No training, huh?'

'No.'

'Sleep well?'

'Yep.'

'You want some toast? Chocolate?'

Lori nodded, and he put some milk in the saucepan, placed it on the heat. She watched him get the powder out and put it in the mug.

She moved closer to the woodstove where the flames flickered behind the glass. Her father carried over the hot chocolate.

'Thanks.' Lori put the mug on the table. 'Dad,' she said. 'Why did we move here?'

'There was money to be earned.'

'Don't you miss home?'

'Not really.'

'D'you wish we could visit more?'

'There's always the phone, or letters.'

'You don't write letters.'

Her father laughed. 'I know.'

'Do you think we'll move again?'

'Don't look like it.'

Lori watched the flames for a while.

'Dad,' she said. 'What did you think when we were born here?'

Her father shrugged. 'Didn't think nothing special. You got to be born somewhere.' He pointed at the hot chocolate. 'Drink up.'

Lori walked from their house to the local store. It was a still, silent day, and every sound travelled as clearly as gunshot, cracking through the air. A dog barked, a snowmobile left for the lake.

The silence returned and it was just her, Lori. She could hear her own breathing and the sound of the snow, being driven right into the tread of her boots.

She passed through the quiet streets and approached the store. Posters in the window announced that week's special offers. But instead of entering through the glass doors, she walked on, right along the next two streets, till she passed the last houses and reached open countryside.

The road led west, out towards the rest of Canada: she had only gone along it twice, both times to visit family. It was a nine-hour drive, full of potholes, like a dirt track. There were only two roads in the whole of Labrador, her father would say. Two roads and neither of them joined up.

Lori looked out over the dark green trees and the snow. The vast blue sky. The one road. She breathed in deeply. There was so much air here.

She entered the glass doors of the store and pulled down her hood. The air was warm, and there was music coming from the tinny speaker in the far corner.

The woman behind the cash desk wore her hair in tight curls, and her glasses half-way down her nose where she was reading one of the store's flown-in magazines. She looked up and smiled. 'Hi, Lori. How's your dad?'

'Good, thanks.'

'Kaylie said you did the two lengths.'

Lori nodded.

'Good pair of lungs on you. Bet your dad was pleased.'

Lori shrugged. 'I forgot to tell him.'

'Oh, Lori, how could you? You run right home now and make sure you tell him. He's so proud of you girls, loves all your news. He's always telling folks what you're up to.'

Lori nodded.

'You promise to tell him now?'

'I promise.'

Lori walked away from the counter and looked around the shelves. She looked at the few vegetables they sold: the bags of potatoes, swedes, carrots and onions. She looked at the cat food, the rows of snacks. Then she turned into the aisle with the bathroom products. She saw the tampons and thought she ought to buy her own box for home, just in case. It couldn't be long now. But then she looked over at Kaylie's mum on the till. She imagined carrying them up to the counter. So, Lori, she'd say, you started then? I see you've chosen the tampons. You'll need those for synchro.

She turned to go and get the milk from the cooler, when she saw the shelf of diapers, baby food and plastic rattles. There was a small rail of vests dangling from white hangers, and she fingered one of them. The fabric was soft and there were three fasteners along the bottom.

Her father was in the garage when she got back, wearing yellow waterproofs, carving the caribou into joints to put in the freezer. The smell rose up: blood and iron and fresh flesh. The concrete floor was smeared with red. Lori could hear the knife cutting through muscle, snagging on tendons. She rushed past and went into the kitchen.

Janine stood by the woodstove, dressed in tight leggings and a tee shirt. Her belly stuck out and she stood with her hands in the small of her back.

Lori stood and stared at her. 'He'll see,' she hissed.

'I know,' Janine said.

Lori heard her father in the garage, throwing the dead weight of the carcass down onto the concrete floor. Janine took the milk from her.

'You want some chocolate?'

Lori shook her head.

Janine picked up the saucepan and carefully opened the carton of milk.

Lori heard the door handle into the kitchen start to turn. She took a last look at the bare strip of belly between Janine's leggings and tee shirt, and she turned and fled the kitchen, ran up the stairs and into her bedroom.

She closed the door carefully and sat on the side of the bed and tried not to think about what would be said downstairs.

She picked up the globe and cradled it in both hands. All those countries, all those places to live. She thought of the charts with arrows to show the way the winds travelled around the earth, and wondered if there was one for people, to show how they had been scattered and settled, some of them – all those years ago – ending up in the cold north, borrowing the furs of animals to keep warm.

And the animals too had scattered, some of them leaving the safety of land, slipping into seas and lakes where their lungs developed into gills, and they could breathe effortlessly under the water.

Yes, all of them – people, animals – were moving around the globe, adapting to where they lived. That was why she, Lori, lived here, with the brutal winds and clear ringing air. She had been blown here and landed in the snow. And that was just the way it was.

Reading Between the Lines

Jane Elizabeth Varley

Jane Elizabeth Varley was married and divorced by the time she was thirty, and spent several tough years as a single parent. Now remarried, Jane has a baby daughter as well as a seventeen-year-old son. She divides her time between London and Ohio. She is the author of three bestselling novels, *Wives and Lovers*, *Husbands and Other Lovers* and *The Truth about Love*. Her latest novel is *Dearest Rivals*, published by Orion. Jane has donated her fee for her story to the Chicique Hospital in Mozambique.

Jeff says that our New Year's Party is a veritable tradition. We've held it for the last fifteen years. It is known as the Forsters' New Year's Brunch and people make quite an effort. Our house is filled with men in cashmere sweaters and women in LK Bennett kitten heels drinking Waitrose champagne too quickly.

Privately, as I squeeze round the living room topping up glasses, I think to myself that the stiff white card invitations should say Liz Forster's New Year's Brunch because I am the one who organises the whole event.

If you have ever thrown this type of party you will know that it is a lot of work. I have draped a fir garland across the black marble fireplace, lugged in the step-ladder to pin glass snowflakes on invisible threads from the ceiling, and dotted the room with bowls of gold-sprayed pinecones, dishes of wrapped Lindt truffles and a basket of huge walnuts and Brazils.

Under the tree there are late presents for the small children, wrapped in white tissue paper printed with little silver Christmas trees. I love finding little peek-a-boo books and wooden cars; miniature rag dolls and painted nutcracker soldiers. The children themselves have been tempted into the playroom with pizza and the Playstation.

But this is the last time Jeff and I will be together on New Year's Day. I put on my best hostess smile and continue round. None of the guests know that it is actually the Forsters' Last Ever New Year's Brunch. I think it would put a damper on things if they did.

My husband Jeff is making no effort to help me answer the door or introduce guests. There are about twenty-five now and I'm expecting another ten. He is wearing his baggy brown moleskins and a sweatshirt given to him at Christmas by his sister. It says *Careful, or you'll end up in my novel*. Jeff hasn't cut his hair for eighteen months now so he looks quite like a hippy – which sits a little oddly with his portly frame and ruddy cheeks.

I pause to chat for a moment to the Dawsons – she newly arrived in Oxhampton, both of them sharp-faced solicitors. It is a second marriage for him and he has brought his daughter who is soon to start at my school. So we chat about four-year-old Emma, all of us carefully avoiding the topic of

Emma's mother to whom he was still married when he met the second Mrs Dawson.

I would never become a step-mother. I have seen too many of them in my years of teaching to know that theirs is a thankless task. After three minutes I make my excuses and chivvy Jeff to answer the door. He puts down his glass and does a mock salute. Nowadays Jeff is determined to challenge convention.

It was just over two years ago that Jeff arrived home from work and announced that he had taken early retirement from the bank. Anna and I exchanged shocked glances. She was doing her Macbeth homework at the kitchen table and I was making Delia Smith's Hungarian goulash. Jeff had mentioned retirement as an option but only casually after a few drinks. Next Jeff sat down, flung off his tie and dramatically tossed it on the ground. 'I'm going to become a writer.'

Anna looked up. 'But you don't know anything about it, Dad.'

Jeff sulked for two days after Anna's tactless but honest remark.

On Sunday he called a family meeting. 'I have made some resolutions,' he announced. 'First, I am going to construct a writer's studio in the garden. A room of my own,' he added.

'Virginia Woolf,' Anna chipped in.

Jeff ignored her. 'Next, I am going to join a

writers' group. I need a supportive environment,' he said in a wounded tone.

Jeff has answered the door, left it ajar and ambled over to the Christmas tree to join the members of the Oxhampton Writers' Group. There is Alex who smokes dope and writes about young people and drugs; Gerald the computer programmer who specialises in sci-fi; and Bernadette who draws inspiration from her days as a nurse in the 1960s' NHS. And Penny, of course. I expect my party will appear in fictionalised form in some of their work. They 'read and supportively critique' each other's writing on the second and last Fridays of the month in the community room at Oxhampton public library.

Penny is the chairperson of the group. She wears her grey hair in a ponytail and has an extensive wardrobe of below the knee skirts in corduroy earth tones. She is married to Peter, a chartered accountant who spends a lot of time away from home doing audits. He makes very good money, it's his own company, and that's allowed Penny to do pretty much what she wants all her married life. She has a Diploma in Counselling but doesn't practise. They have no children, only cats.

Penny, I gather, writes contemporary fiction with overtones of social commentary. I wonder what she would say about me?

Liz Forster, a heavy-set woman in her mid-forties

wearing too much make-up, teetered round her bourgeois living room. The room looked out onto a 200-foot garden, Liz's pride and joy. There was enough land there to house several families in eco-friendly structures. To the casual observer Liz was mingling happily enough with her guests (none of whom gave any thought to how the money spent on this so-called celebration might more usefully have been spent). But those perceptive souls with an interest in psychoanalysis would note that she kept all conversations to a polite minimum. It was as if she was afraid of saying too much . . .

I turn up the light jazz playing in the background. From the dining room comes the sound of happy eaters clustered round the buffet – glazed ham, potatoes boulangère, and a pumpkin risotto for the vegetarians. As I congratulate the deputy head's wife on the news of her pregnancy – after years of IVF and they're very excited – I see out of the corner of my eye that Teresa, our neighbourhood watch co-ordinator, has arrived.

Teresa was most concerned when Jeff submitted the planning application for The Studio. She appeared at our front door with a photocopy of the architect's plans.

'But he's already got a study in the house,' she said, puzzled.

'Yes,' I explained, 'But apparently he needs solitude.'

Teresa gave her reluctant blessing to the project and turned her attention to the fund to re-roof the parish hall. The Studio was duly built, equipped with electricity, heating and all-new John Lewis furniture. Jeff got very engrossed in the details: it was impossible for him to start writing until the right ambience had been achieved. The desk was situated by the window to assist creativity. Along the wall, framed photographs of the greats of twentieth-century literature appeared: George Orwell is nearest to the window and T.S. Eliot and D.H. Lawrence are in the middle. There was only room for one more on account of the floor-to-ceiling bookshelves so Harold Pinter went up and Kingsley Amis got moved to our downstairs loo. On the opposite wall, above the sofa, is the Hay-on-Wye literary festival poster Jeff brought back from the Oxhampton Writers' Group trip. The trip only lasted two days but an awful lot happened while they were away. On the windowsill is the small china bust of Dickens, a studio-warming present from Penny.

I go into the dining room to check on the state of the buffet. It is half-intact but the second dish of potatoes will be needed after all. I hurry into the kitchen where my friend Maggie finds me. Maggie lives in the Grange, a newish development of five bedroom, five bathroom houses.

'How are you feeling?' she asks solicitously.

'I'm fine,' I say. I am. I feel surprisingly calm.

She whispers, 'I don't know how you can do it. You must have nerves of steel.'

Do I? I have always been very organised I suppose. Which in my experience means concentrating on the task at hand. I teach at Oxhampton primary school, Year Two, and it isn't the sort of job for someone who is easily ruffled. If I say it myself I am very popular. Many of my old pupils still write to me. At Christmas I get bottles of good wine from the parents and even the occasional Jo Malone gift basket which is my favourite. Oxhampton, you will have gathered, is a prosperous middle-class town with a Farmers' Market and an Arts Festival.

Maggie refills her glass and offers me one. I shake my head. I need to have my wits about me for what is soon to come.

Jeff's first novel was a financial thriller based on his years in the City of London. 'Write about what you know,' he said, several times. Jeff decided to write in longhand with a Mont Blanc ink pen using bound notebooks purchased from a legal stationers in Chancery Lane. Jeff reported that the group went wild about *A Share of the Proceeds*. Alex said that it was just the thing for the retired *Daily Telegraph* reader and Bernadette said it was scrupulously researched.

There is a distant thud and scream from the

playroom. I dash along the hallway to find Emma, the Dawson's four-year-old, holding her knee. I scoop her up and soothe her and carry her to the party and the arms of her father. His wife appears anxious but swiftly stands aside to allow Mr Dawson to down his glass and sit with his whimpering daughter. It is a myth that women are naturally caring.

A Share of the Proceeds ground to a halt at Chapter Three. Jeff diagnosed himself with writer's block and purchased an Italian espresso machine to cure the problem: all those trips into the house for coffee were fatal to the concentration. But neither the espresso machine nor the new leather-bound 'ideas and inspiration notebook' did the trick. History, it turned out, had always been Jeff's first love and so he put the thriller aside. He would put it safely in a drawer and return to it at a later date. Then he began *Cloisters and Clues,* his medieval monk murder-mystery.

I think everyone has arrived now. The dining room is looking pretty full, a stack of plates gathered up by Maggie has appeared in the kitchen and Mrs Dawson is deep in conversation with Peter while her husband holds thumb-sucking Emma on the sofa. As I pass by I hear Peter talking about VAT.

It was quite by accident that I met Peter in Oxhampton Waitrose on a Saturday morning. Previously we had met only once before at the writers' group Christmas pub lunch for significant others. I think of all the members of the writers' group, Bernadette the ex-nurse would write the best account. Jeff and Penny agree that Bernadette is a hopeless cause.

Liz and Peter bumped into each other by the jams and preserves. Instantaneously Liz was blind and deaf to the hustle and bustle of the gay Saturday morning shoppers. The expression of brooding misery on Peter's face made Liz transfixed like a statue.

'I think we need to talk,' said Peter morosely after a timeless and agonising pause. 'There's something you need to know.'

'What is it?' said Liz. Liz felt a wave of fear strangulate every fibre of her being. She forgot completely that she had run out of marmalade.

'We can't talk here,' said Peter looking over each shoulder. He looked as if he was afraid that he would be overheard by someone.

'Why don't we go to the Copper Kettle and talk about it? We could order two cups of coffee and two toasted teacakes,' said Liz.

Maggie had already been dropping hints. 'They do spend a lot of time together, Liz.' So Peter's concerns hardly came as a surprise to me. Peter began by blaming himself. 'I'm away so much, you see. Penny's always struggled to find things to occupy herself. The jobs always end up badly. Before the writing it was the yoga teacher's course . . .'

Maggie suggested not inviting Penny and Peter to the party but that would only have aroused Jeff's suspicions. I needed time to make arrangements. I didn't want Jeff to steal a march on me. He might claim to have renounced material things but I don't believe that for one second.

I look around the living room. Maggie's two alluring teenage daughters are looking bored. Teresa the neighbourhood watch co-ordinator has captured Maggie's husband in the corner. I am irritated to see that Jeff is still standing with Penny, Alex, Bernadette and Gerald – though they all ignore Gerald, the self-employed software programmer and treasurer of the writers' group. Gerald lives alone and has somewhat limited social skills. Just then I notice Alex slip away from the group, go into the kitchen and then I hear the sound of the door closing. He's the one who writes about drugs and I can guess what he's up to.

Soon after Jeff joined the group we were invited to Penny's summer barbecue, apparently the high point of the Oxhampton arts community's social calendar. Jeff insisted on staying behind to smoke dope with Alex. I got a call at about ten o'clock the next morning from Penny to come and collect him. I found him very much the worse for wear in Penny's spare room with a damp flannel over his head. Peter, who is six foot and a former rugby player, had to virtually carry him down the stairs. Jeff never smoked dope again. Instead he made do with wearing the hemp sweater that he got from the Oxhampton Farmers' Market. It's grey with leather patches on the elbows.

Jeff, Penny and Bernadette have huddled together and I have the feeling that they are talking about Alex. The recent news of Alex's two-book publishing deal with Random House for *Crystal: The Journal of an Amphetamine Addict* has caused a few ripples in the writers' group. 'It's total rubbish,' shouted Jeff bitterly that Friday night, opening a bottle of Merlot. 'He's not even a real junkie. Hell, maybe I should write about shooting up and burgling chemists' shops. This country is for philistines.'

Jeff abandoned *Clues and Cloisters* soon afterwards and began his children's book. 'It's the only genre where quality still has a place,' he said shaking his head sadly. On Day One – pristine notebook, fresh ink cartridge – he printed out a new affirmation and pinned it to his corkboard:

JK Rowling

Here I come!!!

The *Frog in the Pond* is an old-fashioned tale of Hoppy and his friends, caterpillar, grasshopper and butterfly. The pond, Jeff explained to me, is an allegory for the world at large. It was apparently Penny's suggestion to add Mrs Snail, a fat housewife figure who moves slowly around the grass perimeter of the pond nagging everyone else to tidy up.

Jeff started it last summer. He felt it was the right time to write a book attuned to the natural world and he bought a pair of green Crocs to celebrate. Anna refused to be seen with him. I think it was with some relief that she set off for her gap year in Australia. 'Will you be all right, Mum?' she said worriedly.

'Oh I'll be fine,' I assured her. Things hadn't reached a point of no return at that point, you see.

An hour later Teresa passes me on her way out of the dining room with a slice of tarte tatin. 'Lovely spread.' She turns and her eye falls on Penny. She moves in closer and whispers softly in my ear. 'It must have taken a lot of guts to hold this party, Liz.' And then she is gone. Of course. Using the cover story of enforcing the neighbourhood watch, Teresa discovers everyone's business and it was stupid of me to suppose that she would be unaware of the affair. I take a deep breath and go to rescue Gerald who has been abandoned by the rest of the group to stand on his own looking out of the window. I take his arm and lead him over to Peter and Mrs Dawson. As I introduce him, I hear Jeff's mildly drunken voice ring out. 'Liz, come here a minute.' My heart misses a beat. I really don't want to talk to Jeff and Penny. 'Liz!' Jeff repeats insistently.

I take a deep breath. I gather all my energy to shoot Penny my warmest smile. The smile she shoots back is equally fulsome.

Jeff sounds effusive. 'Penny was saying that she and Peter are renting a house in the Dordogne this summer. She's invited us!'

'It's the most beautiful part of France,' cuts in Penny.

'Very inspiring,' interrupts Jeff.

'Great,' I lie. I surprise myself as I have done so many times in the past eighteen months.

'Sounds fabulous.' Even though I know there will be no holiday, I add earnestly, 'Do let us have the dates.'

I am saved by Maggie appearing at my shoulder. 'Liz, I think you need to check on the cherry pie.'

I do not. It is sitting perfectly happily on the dining room table where Maggie put it half an hour earlier. But Maggie is anxious that I do not betray myself. As she steers me towards the kitchen she repeats to herself, 'I do not know how you do it.'

Anna called me from Adelaide and offered to fly home for Christmas. 'Mum, I worry about you.'

But much as I wanted her to, I took a deep breath, put on my best no-nonsense voice and put her off. 'It's not worth it, is it? And you'll want to be in Sydney for New Year won't you, with all your friends?' It's best that she's not around when I announce what I know.

Maggie does not need to worry; I will wait until the time is right.

The guests have reached that stage of helping themselves to drinks in the kitchen. I would quite like to go upstairs, put on my pyjamas, climb into bed and eat a chocolate orange. I do online Weight Watchers and in the last year I have lost a stone, two to go, which Maggie attributes to the stress of dealing with the 'Jeff-Penny-Peter situation'. I think Peter copes by concentrating on his work. Penny, of course, behaves as though nothing is amiss. For someone with a supposedly artistic temperament she is extraordinarily insensitive to the feelings of those around her.

My guests leave late, which I take as a compliment. Jeff has come to stand by the door to take the credit. Penny and Peter kiss both of us goodbye. As they thank us, I wonder how our other guests will react to the news. I suppose they will take sides: the wronged wife will garner the most sympathy but not many invitations. As for the cheating husband he will be condemned but forgiven in time. I don't expect it will put Jeff off his writing for long. Who knows, it might give him the inspiration he needs. I close the door on the last guest and ask Jeff to come into the kitchen. Yes, it could bring forth yet another new novel: *Diary of a Newly Divorced Man*.

Jeff was in a state of shock and very possibly in need of urgent medical attention. But his years in the City of London had taught him to stay cool under pressure. Jeff also possessed the intellectual skills of an Oxford professor and the quick wits of a secret service agent.

Jeff had been totally unprepared for the news of his wife's shocking betrayal.

Cruelly, she chose the day of their New Year's Eve Brunch – a veritable tradition – to disclose her treachery. 'Jeff, it's over. I'm leaving you for someone else,' she said bluntly.

'What?'

'I'm leaving you.'

'What?'

She did not trouble to hide her impatience. 'I'm leaving you for Peter! Haven't you guessed by now?'

Jeff called her a number of unrepeatable names which were wholly justified. 'Get out of my house,' he shouted very reasonably.

She laughed. 'No, Jeff. You can get out. Why don't you go and sleep in your precious studio?'

Now, after constructing a makeshift bed on his sofa, Jeff lay down and planned his next move.

Poor Jeff. He really had no idea. Neither will Penny. That's the trouble with these writer types. They can't see any further than the end of their pen. Peter and I first slept together when they were away at Hay-on-Wye. After that it was easy. What with Peter's audit obligations and my school holidays, opportunity was never a problem. Peter is the man Jeff used to be: quiet, unassuming, reliable, a good provider and well able to keep me in parties, stiff white card invitations and Waitrose champagne.

Oh, did you think a primary school teacher didn't have expensive tastes? Good Lord, how much do you think this party cost? Clearly you haven't been paying attention. I expect you didn't stop to wonder how we were managing on Jeff's pension or how much that bloody studio came to or how we were going to pay for Anna to go to university.

I think you misjudged me. I worry that you may be a bit like Jeff. I have wants and needs as well. If you were hoping for some soap opera showdown at the end of the party when I publicly denounced Jeff as an adulterer and Penny as his mistress then you are to be disappointed. For a start I don't think they have ever been lovers. Poor Penny loves her husband. I say poor Penny. I do feel guilty but I don't really have any sympathy for her. She should have paid more attention to him. Did you notice how I foisted Gerald on Mrs Dawson who was getting just a little too cosy with Peter?

Peter is telling Penny right now. In a few days, after Jeff cracks under the psychological pressure and moves out, Peter will join me here. I'm good at getting people to do what I want. I have that knack of making people want to please me. I can't teach it to you – you've either got it or you haven't. As I look around the kitchen I notice that Maggie has already done most of the clearing up.

So Peter and I will live in this house, Anna will

come home for the holidays and we will all get on just fine. My solicitor has all the papers drawn up and I'm well ahead of the game.

Next year there will be the New Year's Brunch just like always. And I'm confident that most of my guests will return. It *is* a fabulous party.

If you were one of my guests I'm sure you would come. You'd tell yourself that Liz's private life is her own affair and only the parties involved know what really happened. Then you'd go shopping for something nice to bring me. You've heard I like Jo Malone.

Unless you're like Jeff. Yes, I do worry about that. In which case I advise you to stop reading right now and start paying close attention to what those around you have been doing while you've had your nose in a book.

Sugar Daddy

Kathy Lette

Kathy Lette has written ten international best sellers. Her latest is *How To Kill Your Husband – and other handy household hints.* She lives in London.

Henry Trump was a self-made man – and he wanted everyone to know the recipe. His wife of twenty years accepted his workaholic egotism. Jenny knew that men were the narcissists; not women. After all, as she wryly informed her girlfriends, men don't think they need make-up!

Jennifer also knew that she was plain. 'Plain? Good God,' she'd giggle, 'I've seen better heads on a pimple.' But pining for beauty beyond her genetic inheritance had no interest for her at all. She just seemed to be missing the vital intellectual capabilities that compel women to be riveted by the minute deterioration details of their skin's elasticity. Busy with her charity work, she had no time to botox or bikini wax; the woman didn't even weed her eyebrows until the Council sent her a public safety letter about over-hang . . . Until, that is, her husband began an affair with a pert and pretty model he met when she was hired for a car campaign by his advertising company. Jenny knew

Chantelle was a Sabre-Toothed Husband Hunter the minute they met at the office party.

'It must be lovely having such small breasts,' Chantelle had purred to Jenny, 'clothes must hang so well. I wish men would respect me for my intellect,' she added, once Jenny had picked her jaw up off the floor. 'If only I could make myself less desirable . . .' She looked Jenny up and down before meowing, 'So, tell me Jen, how do *you* do it?'

When Chantelle inquired what Jenny did for a living, her husband, Henry, informed the model that Jenny gave up her career as a doctor to devote herself to her family and was now just as deeply devoted to their grandchildren.

'Oh, how lovely to do nothing!' chirruped the Sabre-Toothed Husband Hunter in reply. 'I know that if I had such a brilliant, successful, incredibly sexy husband, I would positively *slave* for him day and night! I wouldn't have time for kids!'

Henry had positively drooled – not a good look on a sixty-three-year-old man. Jenny merely sighed. Men are so easy to flatter – she told her girlfriends later, you just tell them what they already think of themselves. And so Jenny had laughed off the model as a transitory attraction. Except that the model soon became more adherent than a Stay-fresh mini pad.

'Of course he's bonking her,' her best friend Victoria warned her as they spied on them through the window of the Caprice, where Henry had taken the model for lunch. Victoria Bollingbrook was cut from the same tweedy mixture of practicality and no-nonsense that supplied the warp and weft of the colonial empire. 'Behind every successful man is a wife and underneath every successful man is a mistress,' she adjudicated, matter-of-factly.

'Otherwise known as a mattress,' Jenny muttered, miserably, as they watched Chantelle spooning crème brulée into Henry's eager mouth.

'But he's on the Atkins!' Jenny whelped. She knew that men were prone to sexual incontinence, that didn't surprise or upset her. She was old enough to know that boys will be boys – and so will a lot of middle-aged men who should know better. What she felt totally betrayed by was her husband's gastronomic infidelity. All those protein-only meals she'd been carefully concocting, all that time-consuming calorie counting in her fat-free kitchen.

'The Atkins? The Fatkins, more like it,' Victoria added caustically.

Henry had always complained that, as the school swot, he'd had no childhood. Well, he was certainly making up for it now. He started listening to the Arctic Monkeys. He discarded his boxers and began 'going commando'. He had his aura toned. He took to drinking full-fat café mocha lattes.

Jenny, who loved her husband, was so health

conscious, so keen to keep her hubby slim and trim, that she wouldn't even cook with thick-bottomed saucepans. Henry, on the other hand, took to devouring three-course lunches at the Savoy Grill, Simpson's Carvery, Rules Restaurant or the Ritz on a daily basis, with particular devotion to the dessert trolley. Oh, how they giggled over their gateaux. Oh, how they simpered over their soufflés. Oh, how they flirted over flambéed peaches in champagne sauce. Henry began piling on the pounds.

Chantelle, however, remained all gymed and slimmed.

'How can anyone possibly get into such a tight pair of pants?' Victoria marvelled.

'Oh, a glass of champagne usually does the tick,' Jenny observed, tartly. Unless the model was keeping her internal organs in her handbag, she obviously had been following the Karen Carpenter Fabulous Tips to a Thinner You. As a trained doctor, Jenny's instinct was to feel concern for the young woman's anorexia. But as the only thing she did seem to devour was men, it was hard to dredge up the compassion for the man-eating predator. Psychologists would no doubt maintain that there was a thin person inside Chantelle trying to get out, but the ruthless model had obviously eaten her.

'Chantelle says that Doctor Atkins died of a brain haemorrhage from lack of fatty acids,' Henry snapped when Jenny confronted him about his expanding waistline. 'She says that you're trying to kill me with all your macrobiotics and mung beans.'

At least Jenny now knew how beautiful bulimics like Chantelle get themselves to throw up – *they just listen to themselves talk.* 'What's the point of being all trimmed and slimmed and gymed if she needs a personality trainer to keep her mental muscles in shape?' Jenny retaliated. 'The woman's intellect had become as starved as her body. I'd be surprised if she could play remedial Scrabble. Or even . . . "Join the *dot*".'

When Henry refused to laugh along with her jibes, Jenny finally realised that her wife warranty was running out; that she was perhaps passing her amuse-by date and would soon be traded in for a younger model. 'You're letting yourself go,' Henry told Jenny, sternly. 'I offered to pay for your face lift, but no! Truth is, you want to look like a wrinkly prune.'

'They're not wrinkles, they're laugh lines,' Jenny replied, fondly, hiding her hurt and humiliation.

'Nothing's *that* funny, Jennifer.'

'What I'm laughing at is you making such a fool of yourself over a bimbo,' Jenny said, seriously. 'Besides, we average women have a role to play. Without us, the beautiful people wouldn't look quite so beautiful,' she quipped, making one last stab at jocularity, 'Henry darling . . . I know you've been acting the goat, but I do still love you so, despite it all.'

But it wasn't love that was in the air, just the car

exhaust of his Alfa Romeo as he sped off into the city sunset with Chantelle. It seemed that Henry's wedding vows read: 'Till Death Do Us Part . . . Or Till Someone Younger Comes Along'. As soon as the divorce came through, he married the twenty-five-year-old Sabre-Toothed Husband Hunter.

'That's the trouble with self-made men,' Victoria comforted Jenny, over their second bottle of wine. 'They worship their creators . . . You know Jen, you are still a very good looking woman,' Victoria reassured her. 'The only thing Chantelle's got going for her is youth. Why not have just a few nips 'n' tucks? Eyes tightened, boobs jacked up, legs lippoed. Little things which look natural.'

Despite the lack of logic to that remark, Jenny did find herself becoming worryingly susceptible to promises of goddess-like transformations. She suddenly found herself looking at magazine ads promoting collagen injections for the mouth. But knowing her luck, she would merely end up looking like those tribal women on the Discovery channel with plates in their bottom lips. Insomniacal with despair, she was often late-night channel surfing, flicking from one bad B-grade movie to another, which is how she was exposed to the advertisements for liposuction. But what would she do with all the fat sucked out of her thighs? Perhaps she could have it sculpted into a statuette for Horrid Henry? Maybe that explained *The Blob*, she pondered, the only movie on at four in the morning. It was merely liposuctioned fat, running free. But a grim realisation started to gnaw and nag at her. Even if she did undergo cosmetic surgery to win back her husband, why would she want a man who only wanted her because she was silicone from teeth to toenails? Jenny surmised that there was only one thing gushing out of the fountain of youth. Money. A sewer of youth was a better description. She informed Victoria that she refused to succumb to society's narrow view of perfection. 'Flaws are so much more interesting.'

'Parquet or linoleum?' Victoria retorted, but gallantly resisted making any jibes about the floor being the only thing which would get laid in her house if Jenny didn't Do Something. But, as a doctor, Jenny was adamant that, on the integrity scale, operating on people who didn't really need it, ranked cosmetic surgeons right down there with syphilitic ulcers and Republican politicians.

Victoria had recently retired from teaching so had all the time in the world to help Jenny spy on the newly weds, who seemed to have taken to the good life like champagne off a duck's back.

'What are they eating tonight?' Jenny would ask, unable to bring herself to peer through the window of the Cipriani.

'A pagoda of profiteroles,' Victoria droolingly reported.

'What is it today?' Jenny asked the next afternoon, unable to take a glimpse through the potted palms of Claridges at the sumptuous cream tea Chantelle was coaxing Henry to tuck into.

'Slowly melting soufflé with hot juicy custard.'

'The way to a man's heart is definitely through his stomach. That is not aiming too high,' Jenny wisecracked to her friends and family, in an attempt to disguise the pain she was feeling.

But what it really was, of course, was a slow form of murder; a legal, lunch-based homicide. Once married, Chantelle took to ordering Henry two desserts – then three, then four. In fact, every sugar-sprinkled, calorie-coated, palate-pleasing, tongue-tickling confectionary the dessert trolley had to offer – ziggurats of zabaglione, glistening towers of tiramisu. Henry's married male friends presumed Chantelle had added spice to his sex life, but the only thing this man wanted whipped was his cream.

Victoria suggested that Jenny use her divorce settlement for some facial resurfacing so that she could find herself another husband. But Jenny remained convinced women only became more beautiful if they read a book now and then. She rejoined the British Library. Now that she was no longer tethered to the stove by her apron strings, painstakingly weighing Henry's food and straining off all the fat, she also had time to sign up to her local book club. And the books she started reading were about Cleopatra and Mata Hari, both of whom were plain with interesting faces – like her. Legend, she realised, was the best cosmetic. You just need to behave like a Goddess to become one, she decided, which gave her the confidence to start a romantic liaison with the thirty-two-year-old librarian she met at book group. And a good bonk, she discovered, gleefully, is much more rejuvenating than a face-lift! Yes, putting a younger man on your menu, may be a form of comfort food – but it is also totally non-fattening!

Nor did she feel jealous any more of the Sabre-Toothed Husband Hunter. Bulimia, after all, will give you a figure to die for – literally. Jenny had also discovered that this wasn't the first time Henry had cheated on her. Oh no. Cleaning out her ex-husband's abandoned study desk drawer, she found old Mars Bar wrappers, crisp packets, fondue fancies, along with the cards of escort girls and massage parlours. It was then she realised that Henry had actually been having a passionate love affair for his whole life – with himself.

When Henry finally had his heart attack, the coroner reported 'natural causes'. But Jenny knew better. It was death by chocolate.

Oh, well, Jenny rationalised as she lay in the arms of her toy boy, that's what happens to a Daddy who likes Sugar.

Cleaning Windows

Nicci Gerrard

Nicci Gerrard has worked with emotionally disturbed children, taught English Literature and Women's Studies on adult education courses, co-founded and edited the magazine *Women's Review,* been a literary editor on the *New Statesman* and *The Observer,* but for the last fifteen years she has been a full-time writer - first on *The Observer*, where she was a feature writer, interviewer, commentator and executive editor, and then as a novelist. With her husband Sean French she has written ten bestselling psychological thrillers under the name of Nicci French, and she has also written three solo novels. She has four children and lives in Suffolk.

There are many things wrong with my face. I don't usually notice them – perhaps I have become invisible to myself over the past few years – but today I saw the grey hairs in my eyebrows, the tiny vertical lines above my upper lip, the frown marks on my brow, the chipped front tooth, the hair that hasn't been cut for – oh, I don't know. Months. I grimaced at my reflection, which suddenly seemed that of a stranger and where had the woman I used to know gone?

The smudge on the mirror had irritated me for weeks. I went to the kitchen and fetched window cleaner and kitchen roll, then returned to the bathroom to spray the mirror and vigorously rub away the mark. As I was doing so, I saw that the window was horribly dirty too. The sun outside was thick and bright, the sky a flawless blue for it was spring, and days were opening up, soft warmth was spreading through the city. It made the grime on the glass very obvious. So I sprayed the window and polished it with the paper towel, but of course most of the dirt was on the outside, a nasty smear caused by car fumes, although the street is not a busy one – the main road is not far off. From here I can hear it. Lorries drive very fast along it, carrying their heavy loads, tipping round corners on their vast tyres. Sometimes at night I wake to hear the screeching of their brakes. Then I can't get back to sleep. I used to try lying quite still in my bed, watching the moon and the stars through the open curtains, attempting to empty my mind. But how can you empty your mind? It's a restless, heaving, sickening thing; it throws up thoughts and rolls images over and over on its foaming waves. Nowadays, I know to get up and make myself a cup of tea and sit in the kitchen to drink it, read a book. Not a novel – it's been some time since I finished a novel – and never poetry either, although Clara and I used to love reading poetry together: every so often, we would learn one off by heart. I remember some of them still ('The sunlight in the garden hardens and grows cold . . .'), though others exist only in fragments. No, I tend to read books about mathematical paradoxes, cosmology, genetics, histories of ages long past; I like lists of fascinating facts. I try and do cryptic crossword puzzles; I am extremely bad at them. I can sit for hours and not get a single answer, although when I check them in the paper the next day they're so obvious. And I have even learnt chess, although I'll never be very good. I don't have the right kind of mind – the one that can think many moves ahead, hold all the alternatives that spread out like capillaries. Never the less I play through famous games and try to learn classic openings. Ross would laugh to hear that, but I don't think I will tell him. I don't think we will have a conversation about end games.

I opened the window wide, so that a gap opened up at its hinge and I could insert an arm holding the bottle, and spray cleaning liquid on its grubby outside surface before tearing off several sheets of kitchen roll. The nearest panes were easy enough, but to reach the further panes I had to drag a chair over and climb up onto the ledge, where I squatted, leaning out to reach the unreachable parts. The problem with cleaning windows is that you can never quite get them pristine. Smears spread; you look at the glass from a different angle and see a different set of smudges; the cleaner one side of the glass gets, the more clearly you can see what you've missed on the other side. My back was aching and my wrist hurt; sweat prickled on my brow. What's more, I noticed that some of the dirt had mysteriously transferred itself to my freshly washed and ironed shirt. Now I would have to change before I left the flat. I needed to look – well, what?

I needed to look as if I was taking care of myself. But it was all right. I had time. I had thought I would walk all the way, stopping at the little café half-way up the hill where we used to eat cooked breakfasts on Sundays, but I could always go by the underground. And I wasn't hungry. I wasn't hungry at all. I tried to remember when I had last eaten. Last night I had made myself a poached egg on toast, but somehow I couldn't manage to swallow it down – I always used to eat poached eggs when I was pregnant and had morning sickness. Poached eggs on crumpets with Marmite, the pierced yolk oozing down through the buttery holes.

The other problem with cleaning windows is that once you've cleaned one, you realise how terribly badly the others need cleaning as well. The sunlight poured in through the bathroom window now, but in the rest of the rooms it was thwarted, polluted. Now I'd begun, I thought, I might as well finish. I took the bottle and kitchen roll through to my bedroom. I still sleep in the double bed and I still sleep on the left-hand side, with my small table, my digital radio, my books of facts and figures, my tube of hand cream, my reading glasses, my mobile phone plugged into its charger. I usually go to bed at eleven, in my red pyjamas that I bought from a catalogue, moisturising cream on my face, and I try to read until twelve. If I am tired enough, I may miss waking in the small hours, when everything is thick with darkness and with dark thoughts. We are made up of our memories. That's what makes us who we are; they are what is most precious in us. But sometimes, in those waking moments, I wish I had no memory at all, that I could wipe it clean with a soft damp cloth and be blank, shiny and new.

This window looks out onto the communal garden. Because it is spring, it is bright with flowers. The daffodils have all gone, but there are tulips, hebes, and honeysuckle climbing up the back wall. There are daisies all over the lawn, and buttercups too. The leaves on the trees have just started unfurling, sticky and light green. As I rubbed at the window with the paper towel, a woman with long, lemon-yellow hair walked out into the garden with a book. She sat on the wooden bench and tipped back her head, eyes shut, to soak in the heat – and when she opened her eyes again, we found we were looking at each other. Then she smiled at me, really smiled as if we were friends who had not seen each other for a long time. I smiled back. I tried to smile back. You know, you have to go on a journey; you have to make yourself take those first steps. Behave in a certain way and then your emotions will follow in the footsteps of your actions. Smile and then you'll feel like smiling; talk and you will start to believe your words. Well, that's what I've often said to other people and now I'm saying it to myself. I'm even saying it out loud; I'm turning into a batty old woman. I think I should get a dog. We used to have a dog, many years ago. An undignified black Labrador with a tail like a whip and a long pink tongue, a crooked crab-like gait, yearning eyes and an excited wet nose. Greedy, cowardly, neurotic, smelly, unconditional. If I got another dog, then I'd take it for long walks, whatever the weather: sloshing through mud following in its feverish wake; throwing sticks into lakes for it to hurl itself at. Or I'd watch telly in the evenings with its warm head on my lap; silky ears and a soft muzzle and a funny little snore rasping in its throat when it slept. I closed the window.

In the kitchen, the sink was full to the brim of peonies: red, pink and white, some opened out in fold after fold of petals, some still thick, tight buds. It's always peonies, bluebells or sweet peas. I had to stand on the surface, among the pans, the scales, the kettle and the juicer, the cracked jug of wooden spoons, to reach the windows. They too face the garden. I leaned out, breathing in the fragrance that rose up, the heady smell of spring. Some of the things in here are new, but some are old and carry with them cherished times. That shallow fruit bowl full of lemons, for instance, with its beautiful smoke-coloured glaze: we bought it in France shortly after we had met. I remember how it felt expensive to us then, though it probably only cost a few francs. It used to sit on the wide window-sill, always with lemons.

The two windows in the living room were completely filthy. The paper towel came away black after a single wipe. I persevered, perforated sheet after sheet gathering up the silt of years. From the street below, I could hear people talking as they walked by. Two young men with shaved heads held hands; as they passed the window, I saw that one had a tattoo of a butterfly on the nape of his neck. An old woman, pulling a nylon shopping basket on wheels, went slowly by. A mother with her little girl. The girl was small and skinny; she had knobbly knees and bony shoulders. She took a skip with every third step, to keep up with her mother. I curled up in the window frame, like a wrong-way-round foetus. 'Darling,' I whispered, my breath puffing a small cloud onto the glass. I put my lips there and left the mark of a kiss, then watched it fade. I didn't know why we still did this. I didn't know if I could manage.

I still had time; I didn't need to leave just yet. I still had time to very quickly clean the other mirrors as well, now I was in the mood. I still had time to polish the small dining table. I dipped a cloth into the tin of wax which comes from Denmark and was very expensive, but brings wood up into a soft and burnished glow.

Suddenly, I was ravenous — hollow and dizzy with hunger. I went into the kitchen and cut myself a piece of brown bread, slightly stale. I put it in the toaster and got out the butter and the marmalade. There were a few crumbs on the surface so I wiped them carefully into the cupped palm of my hand and then shook them into the bin. I never used to be this tidy. Clara and I were always the slobs. Clothes strewn everywhere, damp towels on the floor, apple cores on the table, open books splayed out on the arms of the sofa, mugs half full of coffee or tea dotting the bookshelves and mantelpieces, pencils and pens down the backs of chairs, beds unmade, beads and bangles in tangled piles. Now I am neat. Everything is in place. I wash up as I go along, dry up, put away. I used to lose things as well — keys, wallets, sunglasses. I left a trail behind me wherever I went. Ross used to get so exasperated. Once, he bought me a key that answered if you whistled. We'd go round the house, whistling and trying to hear its beeping response. The trouble was, it used to beep at other thing as well — at a certain tone of voice, laughter, the telephone. I threw it away in the end. Now I try not to lose anything: I am careful. Very very careful. Of course, I don't have much to lose anymore.

The toast popped up and I spread butter over it, thinly, then the marmalade. I took a bite and chewed slowly. Today, it didn't taste right. The marmalade was too bitter and the toast like cardboard. I managed four mouthfuls then threw the rest in the bin. I washed the plate and the knife, replaced the butter and the marmalade.

I still had time to have very quick shower and change into clean clothes. I pulled off my shirt and trousers, my knickers and bra, and stepped under the jet of hot water, careful not to get my hair wet. I soaped myself thoroughly, watched as the sudsy water streamed off my pale skin. I touched my belly with two fingers, touched one breast. How long had it been since someone touched me, loved me? I knew the answer, of course. It had been five years. My dear hearts, my sweetest loves. Hanging off my arm, laughing into my face, holding me tight, knowing the right words. Had I known then how happy I was? Of course not; how could I have done?

I dried myself thoroughly and as I did so I noticed that my toe nails needed cutting. I knew I needed to hurry now, but I got the clipper and, sitting naked on my bedroom floor, methodically snipped a thin crescent off each nail, throwing them one away one by one. I cut my finger nails too, although they didn't really need it. Somehow I wanted to feel pared down, nothing extraneous about me. I put on clean underwear, though I'd only been wearing the old ones for a couple of hours. I chose another pair of trousers, too, dark grey and baggy, and then my favourite white shirt. Putting my face into its cottony folds. I breathed in its clean, ironed smell. A memory engulfed me and I felt my heart swell up inside me, impossibly large and pulpy, like a bruised fruit: sinking my face into another shirt, breathing in the familiar smell, so dear to me. I pulled on flat black pumps, good for walking. I brushed my hair behind my ears.

Standing in front of the long mirror, I examined myself. I straightened my shoulders and held up my chin. I met my own gaze and held it. I looked calm, severe, contained, and I thought that I would do.

In the kitchen, I gathered up the peonies, feeling the rubberiness of their stalks and the silk of their petals, and wrapped them in newspaper, and then put them into a plastic bag. I badly needed to leave now, but still I tarried. Was the oven turned off? Were my door keys in my bag? Did I have my money, my phone? For a moment, I stood in the living room and a sense of utter disorientation came over me. I wanted to curl up in a tight huddle on the floor, wrapping my arms round my knees and tucking my head in, squeezing my eyes shut. I didn't want. I couldn't. I never. I never.

There. I was out of the flat, double-locking the door, then down the stairs, walking briskly, out on to the street where the sun shone down between the office blocks. There was still blossom on some of the trees. People wore bright, light clothes; spring was in their steps. In the miniature park, couples were spread out on tartan rugs. I felt the warmth on my skin, in my hair. Do you remember?

Ross was a few hundred yards from the main entrance, underneath the chestnut tree. It is exactly where he stands on this day every year, waiting for me. He is always there before me, although he has to travel from out of town and it must take him at least two hours: perhaps he arrives a long while before our appointed time and simply stands there like this, not moving. I have never asked him. He was holding a bunch of anemones, jewels of deep blue and red, as he always does. He says that they remind him of you, so bright and sweet. He didn't see me at first, and so I could look at him. I used to know him so well, every move he made, and now he is a stranger – a big-boned, handsome man, well-worn and tousled and creased, with new strands of grey in his dark hair. He makes clothes seem crumpled as soon as he puts them on. He looked kind and tired and not at all impatient at my lateness – but then Ross is a patient man, gentle and a stoic. I have always loved that about him. I used to think that when I was with him I was a better person. That changed, of course (although I always knew it wasn't really his fault, it could just as well have been me and the fact that it wasn't was simply a matter of moral luck) and there came a day when I could no longer bear to be in his presence, could literally not stand to have him near me, but it is still worth remembering. I am quite sure that he is patient and kind with his new wife, whom I have never met, and his two little children. Twin girls, one year old. I wonder, does he compare? Does he? How could he not?

He must have felt me looking at me, because he turned his head and met my gaze. He didn't exactly smile, but his face softened and an expression came into his eyes. It was – how can I describe it? – it was the expression of someone who saw me, knew me, understood me, didn't judge me. It made me feel naked, raw, and for a moment I faltered and almost stopped. But I managed to keep going. I kept my head up and I didn't look away and when I got near he held out his hand. It is what he always does, and I always take it, shifting my flowers to the other arm. We walked like a familiar couple up the last stretch of hill, and into the gates. His hand was strong and warm. I glanced down at it, his strong fingers, clipped nails. I see the wedding band, thick gold and gleaming new. Ours was thinner. I wonder where it is.

We didn't say anything to each other. What could we say? It's a beautiful day isn't it? Did your journey take long? Are you all right? How's your work? How's your health? How are your children? How's your wife? How's your life? We walked along the broad main path for several yards, then turned left down a narrower path. Our feet knew the way to go and our hearts knew the way to go and sometimes I think this is the place where I am happiest, although it is also the place where I am saddest. Two great cross-currents meet and heave against each other. Today, I let myself remember you.

You had tiny hands and tiny feet; you had big grey eyes and freckles across the bridge of your nose which spread in summer; you had tangled copper-coloured hair which I used to put in pigtails, pony tails, French plaits; you had a dirty laugh, even when you were very little; you had scabby knees and a plump tummy and soft downy skin like a peach; you had a stork mark when you were born at the back of your neck, and it never quite faded away, it was still there when . . . When. You liked singing and could hit a true note; you liked climbing trees and could reach the top branch; you liked owls and birds of prey; you liked chocolate digestives and pasta with pesto and lemon ice cream and blue cheese. You had night terrors when you were young and would gallop round the house with your eyes open: I would lead you back to bed and sit beside you stroking your face until you slept again. I stroked your face and I crooned nonsense lullabies. You called me Mummy and no-one will ever call me Mummy again.

At the grave we crouched down – me on your left and Ross on your right. He put the bunch of anemones on the green mound and I took out the peonies and laid them over you. You are my peony, my sweet pea, my bluebell, my honey heart. Ross was crying, as he always cries. Big tears slid down his nice, battered face and he didn't bother to wipe them away, just let them fall, and I heard him saying your name, in the way he always used to say it. Clara. As if you were in the next-door room, concentrating on your drawing with your tongue on your upper lip and a great frown on your face. As if you could hear him. Clara my love?

I didn't cry. I never cry. Ross once asked me why and I just shook my head. I didn't tell him that if I began crying, then I would not stop, not ever. An ocean of tears. I reached out my hand and put it, palm down, on the grass which was warm in this glorious spring sun. I just pressed it down. Sometimes I think I can feel a heart beating there. I think of you, lying out here all alone, in every weather. There was a poet who once wrote about the loved ones who had died: I am rich in all that I have lost. I too am rich in all that I have lost. Cherish precious things.

Ross stood up and held out his hand and I took it and let him pull me to my feet. Our flowers spilled richly over the little grave. We walked back down the path to the gates and then he put his hands on my shoulders and kissed me on both cheeks and he walked away in one direction and I in the other. I walked all the way back to the flat. As I arrived, I looked up and saw the clean and gleaming windows, and your sweet face not there.

Annie's Dictionary

Elizabeth Buchan

Elizabeth Buchan lives in London with her two children and her husband. She read for a double degree in English and History at the University of Kent at Canterbury and began her career as a blurb writer for Penguin Books. This was excellent training for an infant writer as it necessitated reading widely through the Penguin list - fiction and non-fiction. She later became a fiction editor at Random House but decided after a couple of years that she should do what she wished to do: write. For her first two novels, she took as her subject very typical watersheds – the French Revolution (*Daughters of the Storm*) and the Second World War (*Light of the Moon*). The latter followed the fortunes of a woman SOE agent in Occupied France. Her third novel, *Consider the Lily*, is the story of a woman in the Thirties who comes terms with her unhappiness through gardening. *Perfect Love* explored the bargains and accommodations that have to be made in any relationship. *Against Her Nature* reworked Thackeray's *Vanity Fair* set against a backdrop of the Lloyds disasters during the Eighties. They were followed by *Secrets of the Heart* and *Revenge of the Middle Aged Woman*. The latter has sold all over the world and has been made into a television film for CBS. Her latest novels are *The Good Wife*, *That Certain Age* and a follow- up novel to *Revenge of the Middle Aged Woman* entitled *The Second Wife*. She is current working on the novel entitled, *Chiara's Book*.

She walked down the road with a nippy spring wind tugging at her coat and hugged it tighter around her while she thought of the many things which were still to do. Susie's dress needed the hem lengthening, and Nick's shoes were – oh Lord why did small boys grow? – too small and needed replacing.

She had worked hard to put aside a small cache of savings for just such eventualities but, however clever her contrivances, the eventualities had a habit of outmatching the savings. Weekly expenditure two hundred and fifty pounds and not a penny more equalled contentment. Weekly expenditure of two hundred and fifty pounds plus a pair of school shoes did not equal contentment . . . as Charles Dickens' Mrs Micawber might have put it. Not that she grudged the perpetual struggle between the fantasy budget and the real one. It's bracing, she told her mother. Oh, bracing, replied her mother, a trifle grimly. I must look it up in the dictionary. The children were her main preoccupation and she had vowed, many times, to work with her might and main to help them into a good, serene life.

At the bus stop, she propped her bag full of groceries up against the lamppost and anchored it with a foot. She could feel the outlines of the tins of baked beans and tomatoes, and the soft squishy one of the rolled porridge oats. Spaghetti tonight, with a grated carrot salad. The children liked that combo. Or rather, she persuaded herself that she liked to think that they liked it because it's cheap, nutritious and easy. She would prepare the meal watching the evening news because she also thought it was important to keep up. She liked to keep up. She needed to keep up.

To think. Verb: to use one's mind actively.

Later on, she would help Susie and Nick with their prep – Mum, what's a past participle? – clean their shoes, iron, maybe listen to a snatch of something on the radio but, more likely, just fall into bed before it all began again. At the weekend, the children would pack their overnight bags and she would put them on the bus which took them to their father's new house and new wife at the other side of town.

It was not much of a life but, then again, it was. She had her children, she was earning a living as the manager of a school kitchen, and she had a night off once a week to be herself.

To breath. Verb: Use lungs. Live. Take breath. Pause.

The bus drew up and she climbed on board. Not that it was the end of the story. Once the children were older ... fifteen and seventeen, say ... she would get a better job. Perhaps retrain? There were plenty of opportunities at night school and, no doubt, there were grants if she set about asking the right questions. She could take the cooking a stage further but her main ambition was to learn Spanish. Spanish speakers almost dominated the world, especially in South America. Juggling around with words gave her a key to unlock the mysteries of thought and feeling and to unlock them via another language was power indeed. In her weekend breathing moments, she pictured herself bouncing around in local buses in – say – Argentina, peering through the window of her proudly acquired linguistic proficiency in on other lives. No, she had never been short of objectives she wished to achieve but they had been postponed due to circumstances.

When she married Pete, she imagined it would be permanent. (Adjective: intended to last.) Certainly, she had made up her mind it was to be so. So had he. 'Permanent' was a good a word, solid and full of promise, but it had been shredded into 'short-term' and 'transient' by a plethora of disappointments and bad feelings which had grown up between her and Pete. How was it possible for the very best of intentions to be so easily knocked down? Easily, it seemed. He accused her of not really being 'there' for him and, surveying his slackening features, his prospering relationship with the beer and the general air of slight seediness which was creeping over him, she was forced to agree. The 'him' that she was 'not there' for was not the 'him' she had married. To be fair, vice versa applied. The girl Pete married was certainly 'not there'. She had vanished somewhere and she could not be traced.

The bus drew up at Winifrith Street and she descended onto the pavement. She grasped the shopping bag by the handles which had metamorphosed into a millstone and began the walk home up the hill.

'Hi, Mrs Dover,' said a voice.

It was Terence from the newsagent who had popped out to change the posters for the evening newspaper headlines. 'Local Boy Makes Good' was replaced by 'Disastrous Flood' and the former's brief reign of glory came to an end in the litter bin.

'Had a good day?' he asked.

He knew, and she knew, he didn't really want a proper answer, but it was pleasant to be asked. 'Business good?' she countered.

The bag grew heavier as she trudged up the rise, passing houses that had once been substantial mansions complete with large gardens and mews for the horses. They were now flats and the areas where the carriages had wheeled in and out had been in-filled to the last square inch by the developers.

She swung round the corner into Magenta Road – why magenta she always wants to know? Small and contained, the house came into view. Pete had left her that. The children need continuity, he said. (Noun: state of being continuous, not abrupt.) For which generosity, she had been grateful. Number 73 needed a lot doing to it, mainly in the bathroom whose fittings were ancient. She and Pete had never got round to the Herculean disruption of replacing the cracked enamel basin and ancient bath.

There was a figure sitting on the wall outside the house. At first, she paid it no attention. Being low and wide, it was the kind of wall that people made a habit of sitting on, and she rather liked the fact that it offered a companionable support when a shoe-lace required tying or the breath catching.

As she drew nearer, the figure sharpened into focus. Tanned, tousled hair, long legs in blue jeans, t-shirt and no jacket (in this weather?), reading a newspaper . . . and something atavistic stirred in her. (Noun: reversion to earlier type.) Memories dragging up from deep in the past – as wonderful and joyous as all the best memories should but which also marched smartly alongside the painful and tormenting – as all memories did.

As she approached, he looked up from the paper, folded it neatly, and got to his feet. 'Hallo, Annie,' he said.

'Hallo, Rob,' she answered and burst into tears.

★ ★ ★

Rob and Annie were inseparable from the word go. She was reading English and he was reading Sociology at the University of Leeds. Neither had any money, both were always hungry. Both loved the theatre, walking and red wine. Both disliked fruit cake, sycamore trees in small gardens and yapping dogs. The likes and dislikes were only gradually exposed because, such was the mutual and tearing attraction, they were too busy discovering the physical aspects of the other to bother with the details. In between bouts, they did find time to talk but in generally sweeping terms – about their ambitions, the state of the world, about living the good, serene life. And, once, about the children they would have. The last had not been an entirely satisfactory conversation.

Friends and parents looked on approvingly. 'This is how it should be,' murmured Alice, Annie's mother, who was inclined to the sentimental and to nipping off to early evening performances of rom-coms at the cinema. 'Young love.'

'Young lust, more like,' countered Jack, Annie's considerably more cynical father. But, in the end, even Jack had fallen under the spell cast by such intense feeling. In fact, everyone who witnessed Rob and Annie's happiness found themselves seduced by the spectacle of the lovers and the suggestion of a future filled with contentment and fecundity. It was irresistible. In particular, the happy couple reminded the elders of what, once, they had had, or imagined they had had, and these elders looked on the golden pair with an ill-concealed envy for what they would certainly never have again.

No such regrets threw their shadow over Annie and Rob. They were too young and too busy living the dream, and enjoying each second of it. During the term times, they worked hard – and also played hard. During the vacations they took temporary jobs as close to one another as possible and, on the long vacations, heaved their rucksacks onto their shoulders and took off. In this way, they got to see Thailand, Laos, Australia, Uruguay and, less enticingly, Bournemouth. After that, having graduated in a blaze of congratulations for their respectable degrees, they decided to go to Polzeath.

It was on the beach at Polzeath after an energetic bout of surfing that Rob grew serious. It was a warm day, and the beach was crowded with umbrellas, families and swimmers. Rob towelled himself down, offering Annie the opportunity to appreciate his tanned torso and nice legs. Then he sat down beside her, scooped up a handful of sand and let it drift down onto her back in a gentle rain. 'What are we going to do about the future?' he asked.

'Future,' she murmured sleepily. Then she sat up. 'The future?' A sudden fear gripped her. 'You're not trying to tell me something, are you?'

'No.' There was a pause. 'Well, yes, sort of. The thing is ... I don't want to settle down yet. I want to do a bit more travelling. I've got the taste for it.'

This was a facer for Annie. 'But I've just got the job.' And, indeed, she had accepted a position as a trainee chef at one of the top restaurants in London. The hours were going to be murderous, the pay disgraceful but the opportunity to learn at the elbow of one of the undisputed masters was not to be missed. It was a chance for which she had plotted, planned and had gone through minor hell to obtain. 'I can't give that up.'

'I don't want you to.'

'Then ... what you are you saying?'

He drew closer and put his arm around her sunburnt shoulders. She leant against him trustingly – for Rob was her rock and her life.

'I wish I could explain properly,' he said, haltingly, 'but I can't settle down quite yet. I have to go and see the world a little more.' By now, the implications had sunk in and she made a little sound of pain. 'This doesn't mean the end of us.' He squeezed her shoulders. 'Far from it. It just means we are apart for a little while we do our own thing, then we'll be together.'

'When you say "apart" how long were you thinking of? A couple of months? A year?'

'I don't know.' Rob's gaze rested on the distant horizon where the blue sea gave way to an even bluer sky.

'But why?' she cried. 'Aren't I enough?'

'I don't know why. It's an itch which I can't explain. I don't want to die without seeing more of the world.' He rubbed his hand up and down Annie's arm and the grains of sand bit into her skin. 'You could come too.'

But they both knew that was not going to happen.

Annie's mother cried and swore it was because she would miss Rob. But Annie had a feeling that Alice knew something which she wasn't telling. Something adult and wise.

After she had seen Rob off at the airport on the flight to Borneo – jungle, logging and trekking – Annie made her way home and wept for two solid days. She developed a habit of turning on her laptop early first thing in the morning to check the emails and always looked at it last thing before going to sleep. At first, Rob's messages were as regular as clockwork. They were filled with descriptions of the landscape, and permissible bits of macho posturing – 'It's real hell trekking through tropical forest.' He wrote about spiders as big as plates, the jungle orchestra and of occasional fevers – 'when I was delirious I thought you were beside me' – and he wrote about the great heavy blanket of heat. Always, Rob signed off, 'I will love you for forever.'

Annie's emails gave careful descriptions of velouté sauces, lobster thermidor and *iles flottants*. She described the comings and goings of a busy kitchen in which every spare inch was occupied, and the wisecracks and tantrums which punctuated the day. She told him how pleased she was with her promotion and how she had been promised a second leg-up if she continued the way she was doing. Always, she signed off. 'I will love you forever.'

Forever. Adverb: continually.

One day, nine months or so later, it occurred to Annie that Rob's emails were less frequent and when they did pop onto her screen they were sketchy and hurried. Sometimes, he forgot to send his love. Annie told herself that these little markers were not significant but, on mentioning them to her mother, she could not help but notice her mother's expression which combined resignation, sadness and the infuriating I-knew-this-would-happen.

A whole month went by without an email. Then two months.

'You know,' said her mother, one Sunday afternoon as they drank tea in the kitchen, 'first love isn't always the one that lasts. Did I ever tell you about my friend Sarah?'

She had, and frequently. The story of how Sarah had been abandoned at the altar by her childhood sweetheart had entered family folk lore. Thus, Annie knew perfectly well that her mother was not guilty of a bad memory but was trying in her way to convey a message.

'Come on, Mum, out with it.'

'Listen, Annie. I don't want to say this any more than you wish to hear it. Darling, it's quite likely that Rob might have forgotten about you. I suspect . . . I'm afraid he might have met someone else.' Her mother bit her lip so hard that it whitened. 'I'm afraid you must prepare yourself.' (To prepare. Verb: make ready.) Alice sat with her hands folded in her lap before raising her eyes to look at her daughter. 'You'll meet someone else.'

In truth, Alice had not said anything over which Annie hadn't already agonised. That night, she sobbed herself to sleep: gulping sobs that tore the heart out of her.

Forgotten. Verb: cease to think of. Put out of mind.

When she got up the following morning, Annie did not turn on the laptop and ignored it when she went to bed. In fact, Annie did not check her emails for a week and from then on, only infrequently. As a consequence, it was a Friday before she got to read the email which had come in on the previous Monday. 'Dear Annie. Forgive me. I don't know how to say this but I won't be coming home in the near future.' There followed a fulsome explanation of how Rob hated himself for hurting her but the lure of travelling was too strong. 'The experiences I'm having are strange ones, and intense, and I can't bring myself to swap them. I love you,' he added. 'I will always love you. I want you to know that.'

She sat down and wrote the following reply. 'I can't believe what has happened. The only way I feel I can cope is to say that from, now on, you are dead to me, Rob.'

That night Annie allowed Pete to take her out, drank too much wine and ended up at his place. Three weeks later she rang him. 'Pete, I have something to tell you.' He listened carefully to the unwanted news and succeeded in surprising her. 'I think we should get married.' He cut through her expostulation. 'Listen. I'm thirty and thinking of settling down. I think you're wonderful, and I want to be with you.'

In between the bouts of morning and evening sickness, Annie thought it over. Pete wanted to be with her. Rob did not. A baby was on the way and the word 'forever' had been downgraded to the kind, sensible and solid option.

She and Pete married in a quiet ceremony in a high-waisted dress that did not quite conceal the swelling bump. Her mother cried harder than she had done in *Gone with the Wind* and her father pumped Pete's hand and said, 'I trust you to look after my daughter.'

Throughout the ceremony, the very nice honeymoon in Paris and the first months of her married life, Annie had an odd feeling that she was not quite there. She could see herself, and hear herself, but an essential part of what had made her what she was – a strand of hope and youth – had fought for life and died. The real Annie had gone far, far away, and she suspected that she would never find her again. Nor did she wish to.

But when Susie was born six months later, those particular worries and preoccupations vanished to be replaced by new ones. And, by the time, Nick was born, they had dimmed into an almost imperceptible dissonance.

★ ★ ★

'What are you doing here?' she demanded of Rob, mopping the tears with her free hand.

He hauled a handkerchief out of his pocket and offered it to her. 'What does it look like? I've come back.'

She returned the handkerchief. 'You think you can just turn up after ten years.' She added, 'And three months and two days.'

'Ah,' he said. 'Not so dead to you then?'

'You are.'

He raised an eyebrow which made his lean, brown face look extraordinarily attractive – a lived-in face with plenty of humour. 'Are you going to invite me in?'

She had an unwelcome vision of the state of the house. 'No,' she said. 'It's too awful.'

He actually laughed. 'I shacked up in mud huts. And worse. Frankly, I'm not going to take no for an answer.'

'My husband might be at home,' she lied.

'You don't have a husband. I've checked with your mother who was very chatty, incidentally.'

She made a mental note to kill her mother. 'I'm expecting the children.'

'Fine.'

He picked up her shopping, carried it as easily as a feather up to the front door and waited to be let in. She led him into the kitchen and he heaved the bag onto the table and began to unpack it.

'You can't do that,' she said.

Again the eyebrow went up. 'Why not?'

'You can't just walk out on me, ruin my life, and then walk back in and unpack the shopping.'

'Looks like that's what I'm doing.' He held up the spaghetti. 'Where does this go?'

She sat down with a thump on a chair and dropped her head into her hands and a pulse, which she had never noticed before, began to beat at the side of her head. 'Why did you do it, Rob?'

'The same reason that you married and had children. I needed to get a lot of things out of my system. You wanted children, didn't you?'

At this point there was a shriek of 'Mum' at the front door and the children arrived back from the school run. She gave both a hug, licked a finger, wiped the smudge from Nick's cheek and said far more calmly than she felt. 'I want you to meet Rob who's an old friend. Rob, this is Susie and this is Nick.'

'Hi guys.' His gaze rested on the golden-haired, well-made pair. Then, it shifted back to Annie. There was a shadow in his eyes and Annie knew without being told because she knew that he was thinking: these could have been ours. 'I used to know your mum when she was young. She could dance all night.'

Nick's eyes flew to his mother's face. 'Mum can't do that.'

'She could,' said Rob.

'I have to get their tea,' she said, 'they're hungry.'

'OK. I'll keep them amused.'

As she busied herself in the kitchen, Annie overheard shrieks of laughter coming and sounds of general contentment coming from the next room. How typical of the children to behave well when she wouldn't have minded if, for once, they gave a visitor a bit of grief. (Visitor. Noun: one who calls on a person.) She gritted her teeth and got on with grating the carrot, so thoroughly in fact that she took off a bit of her finger. That made her furious.

She sucked the macerated finger and considered the words with which she would usher Rob out of the door. Then she realised the children had gone quiet and she put her head around the door. The sight which greeted her caused her to catch her breath. Rob was seated on a chair and Nick and Susie were facing him on the sofas and, it was true to say, their mouths were hanging open.

'It was a big python,' he was saying, 'and it had wrapped itself around . . . ' Something alerted him and he looked up at her, smiled and Annie's heart performed a somersault. Painfully aware that she looked every inch of her years, she said, 'You'd better go.'

At the front door, he stopped. 'I feel very at home here. Can't I stay? For a little?'

With her passion and hope, the younger Annie was trying to make herself felt while the older post-naive Annie endeavoured to smother her. 'No, no.'

No. Particle equivalent to negative sentence.

'Why not?' he asked, reasonably and very politely. 'Why not begin again? It's different now, Annie.'

'You went away and left me.'

His hand was on the door knob. 'I certainly did,' he said, 'and I'm the better for it. And so are you.' He peered at her. 'You haven't changed at all, you know.'

'I can't go through all that again.'

'I'm not asking you to go through all that again. I'm home for good. Let's see what happens.'

'Rob, you said forever and look what happened.'

'For goodness sake,' he said impatiently. 'I'm here, Annie. Shall I stay, or shall I go?'

She stared at him. Go? Stay? Forever? Never? Which word to choose? Old life, new life? To her surprise, the old Annie laughed and leant against him. 'What do you think?'

For ever. Adverb: for all future time. (This is distinct from 'forever' cited above.)

Girl Power Revisited

Kate Mosse

Kate Mosse is an author, broadcaster and Co-Founder & Honorary Director of the Orange Broadband Prize for Fiction. She is a guest presenter for Saturday Review, Open Book and A Good Read for BBC Radio 4 and the author of six books, including the international bestsellers *Sepulchre* and *Labyrinth*, both of which are published in 37 countries. *Labyrinth*, which has sold more than 3 million copies worldwide, won Richard & Judy's Best Book at the British Book Awards and was picked as one of Waterstone's Top 25 novels of the past 25 years. Involved in several literacy and reading initiatives, Kate is a judge of the 2008 Penguin/Decibel Prize.

I am ashamed. Still, after all these years. Of all the words I wrote. Of the person I became. It's why I am making this journey in the dying hours of this December afternoon. Up above, at ground level, a chill pink dusk is patterning the sky red over Waterloo Bridge while I sit here, confined, the rattling of the rails in my ears, with a bag filled with memories. In my hands is a record of their lives. Of mine. A shabby, one-sided relationship.

In the papers – yesterday, maybe the day before, I'm not sure – gossip about Baby twisting her ankle. Anxious all week about this pilgrimage, I kept my thoughts busy, my fingers occupied, with the usual day to day and endless newsprint. At breakfast, in the staffroom, home while waiting for the microwave. A small item about authors going to Downing Street to deliver a petition about illiteracy rates in the UK. Reports of the government's plans to transform childhood by 2020. A Labour Minister setting out his blueprint to make kids' lives better in the one breath. In the next, holding up the reunited Spice Girls and Margaret Thatcher as great role models. Crazy. The blink of an eye and it's as if the last ten years never happened. Still, no comprehension, of the unhealthy affair between glossy-eyed celebrity and the lives of real girls, boys, women.

In the comprehensive where I work, I see the hangover of Girl Power everyday, both good and bad. The dark side of false expectations, disappointments, stories too fragile and insubstantial to take the burden. But, there too, is the confidence, the self-possession, the refusal to accept limitations. Two sides of the same coin.

Back then, in 1996, awkward and not quite fitting in, I bought into Girl Power. It seemed something new, different, to be something significant. I had the clothes, bought the records, the dolls, the shoes. All our desires – *my* desires – reflected onto Sporty, Posh, Baby, Scary, Ginger. Five ordinary girls with an extraordinary story. Five normal girls, pretty in a next-door-neighbour way. The original 'once upon a time' brought up to date, a fairytale with a twist. Us, but our better, brighter versions. The girls we could be if we bought into Girl Power.

They say now, the retrospective poison pens, that the Spice Girls were the first manufactured band.

True? Maybe, although it's certainly not how I saw it back then, even when I knew the facts. How, in February 1994, Heart Management placed an advertisement in *The Stage* asking: 'Are you street smart, extrovert, ambitious and able to sing and dance?' Hundreds of girls turned up to show that they were all these things and more. Manufactured? Of the five originals chosen, two didn't survive the cut, or didn't fit in, so they kept looking until they had the perfect line-up. Mel C could sing, Mel B could dance, Posh pouted, Geri strutted, Baby smiled. But once they were together, everything changed. They got a new manager, they were in control, changed the band's name from 'Touch' to 'Spice Girls', and Girl Power hit the ground running. We'd not seen anything like it. Wanted to be part of it.

July 1996, a summer of sunshine and showers, and 'Wannabe' hit the charts. In at No 3, then No 1 for seven weeks. It went on to be not only the biggest-selling debut single ever by an all-female group but also the biggest-selling single by an all-female group of all time. It was the first big story I covered. I'd just left the Tech after a couple of false starts and was new to the paper, stuck on the news desk but aspiring to be a music journalist. I used the hook of having the same birthday as Emma Bunton – that, and the fact I'd grown up in Maidenhead, close to where the girls had lived in their pre-Spice days – to persuade the editor to let me write a review of their first album, *Spice*, in November 1996. Great pop music, great band. My own first taste of Girl Power.

It was love at first sight, the start of a beautiful relationship. There they were, telling girls to go for it. To be who they wanted to be, to do their own thing whatever anybody else said. Telling *me* to go for it. I wasn't just a fan. I didn't model myself on any one of them. We were equals, their lives a mirror to my own. I was independent and ambitious, one foot on the ladder, me and the Spice Girls, on parallel paths. They were more than the sum of their parts – the nicknames, the clothes, Adidas trainers or platform shoes, bunches and lollipops or tattoos and pierced tongues. This was female solidarity in action, friendship, fun. Pop princesses, certainly, but with a message. Be who you want to be. Dress how you want to dress.

I carry the article with me still, in my wallet, as a talisman, a warning. The print is faded, folded, creased. It's both the best and the worst piece I ever did. Looking back, it's amazing how quickly infatuation turned to obsession. I wrote about everything they did – where they were, what they wore, what it meant. Posh, Ginger, Sporty, Baby and Scary's lives were more real to me than my own. Boyfriends came and went, not able to compete.

Nine No 1 singles. I cheered them on, my star rising with theirs. I believed they were holding a mirror up to our changing times. December 1996, the Christmas No 1, 'Two Become One', a ballad that concealed the safe sex message wrapped up in tinsel inside. Clever, tricksy, feminism lite, sure, but none the less important for that. I understood. This was new. Something different.

We all thought it, didn't we? That it was real. Here to stay? Headlines, clichés, suddenly five girls on whom the modern world might depend? Positive role models, not just the same old story in new clothes? They were ourselves given back, but more determined, more definite. Streetwise, sassy, irreverent, girls having it all. Flirting, cheeky. Flouting protocol, Girl Power was seeing Geri Halliwell with Prince Charles. Girl Power was the thousands of screaming fans everywhere they went. Girl Power was footage of the Spice Girls meeting Nelson Mandela.

My reputation, too, grew. I was one of them, proud of them, part of the Girl Power revolution, an expert. I got poached by a national paper and, looking back, that's when the relationship started to turn sour. Just the odd wobble at first. I winced, just a little, when Ginger Spice held up Margaret Thatcher as the original Spice Girl, but only a little. At first. And if I felt just a tiny bit superior to all those pre-teen fans swallowing it all hook, line and sinker, I dressed it as disappointment. We respected Geri's right to an opinion, of course we did – that's what Girl Power was all about – but we couldn't help but worry where it all was heading.

That old British pastime of building people up just to knock them down. They were moving on, moving up, leaving me behind. My pieces became neutral, neither pro nor anti, but lost somewhere in between. And it's funny. Even now, having worked so hard to put it all behind me, I remember all the dates, every tiny detail of the end of our affair. Every second of my life was informed by every minute of theirs. On 5 November 1997, the Spice Girls fired their manager. And I? I, the expert, the leader writer, hadn't seen it happening. It was humiliating. I should have seen the writing on the wall, but I hadn't. I'd missed the exclusive. The Girls had made me look stupid. I toughened up, no longer on their side. Started to file pieces that were neutral, then critical, then spiteful. More in sorrow than anger, such treacherous fingers flying over the keyboard. In the end, what did it all really add up to? It was only pop, not politics. Girl Power was not *real* power. They needed to not cross the line. Know their place.

Our relationship was on the rocks. Two on the way to becoming one. The press pack was snapping its jaws, sharpening its claws, and I joined them. First among equals. My words were tough. About how the Spice Girls owed it all to the manager they'd sacked. They were his creation – *our* creation. They were products not people. A brand not a real band. Ungrateful. Affairs and fights, no smoke without fire. Like all those other ambitious girls trying to impress the boys, I turned on them. I peddled spiteful rumours, I fanned the backlash. The criticism was all the more welcome to the editor because it came from a 'once-upon-a-time fan'. And it got me what I wanted. Not just a by-line in the paper, but a photo too. At last, me and the girls together, side by black and white side. December '97 and, sure, the Spice Girls still went to No 1, but were kept off the Christmas Day slot by the Teletubbies. I knew it was just a matter of time. So I smiled, the Judas smile of a collaborator, when the manager of a boy band, called them 'five old boilers'. I nodded when the *Mirror* asked their readers to vote on which Spice Girl was the Most Irritating. They had it coming.

I was at my cleverest, most witty, most acerbic. In print, at least. The more I belittled and diminished their achievements, the higher my value. Friends drifted away, but I didn't notice. I was out every night, parties, bars. And every week in my column, I tarred and feathered and hounded them, running with the big girls and boys now. Girl Power? A myth. A false dawn. We'd all been tricked. The Spice

Girls weren't good role models. Whose fault was it kids were dressing in clothes too tight, too short, too revealing? Theirs. And far from raising ambition and self-esteem, actually they were encouraging girls to rate looks over brains. Same old, same old. Girl Power? Just licence to drink, to stick your fingers down your throat. Celebrity culture? Down to them and brought direct to your breakfast tables by Kiss & Tell merchants and cheque book journalists.

Then Geri went. May 1998. From *Famous Five* to *Fab Four*. Blyton to comic strip overnight. Less 'Viva Forever' than 'Goodbye'. The news broke the day I was moving house. Another failed relationship, this time one that might have mattered, although I never got round to telling him. Wrapped up in my own drama, taking the edge off with cigarettes and vodka, the precise moment the Spice Girls came crashing down, I was on my knees dividing up the CDs into his pile and mine. Someone else broke the story. *My* story. Someone else's photograph was slapped on the page next to an old shot of Geri in her Union Jack dress. Crash and burn, it was over. For them. For me. For good. My mother said she couldn't make out a word I said on the phone, but she and Dad came and got me all the same and took me home. I was still there at Christmas, the following Easter. A broken heart takes time to mend. Ten years, all told, separating the girl I was then from the woman I am now.

The intervening years have been kinder to me than to you. I got my life back on track in private. I had the chance to start again, to kick the habit of living in your shadow. I grew up. Whereas you? You continued to have your personal lives picked over in public. To be served up for our amusement on the front pages of the tabloids and tatty weeklies. Ten years on and little has changed. The tickets for your reunion gig sold out in 38 seconds, or so the papers say, but you're still easy targets. You still stand accused of being too rich or too thin or too plastic or too false. For all of which read, too successful. All over the papers again, all things to all people, saviours and devils. Girl Power, fact or fiction? The same contempt, the jealousies, the bitterness of the profession which I'm ashamed to have once belonged to. Still, you represent all manner of things, you cannot be simply yourselves.

The next station is North Greenwich. Around me now, in this humming underground carriage, women of a certain age, guys with low-slung jeans, teenagers chic and self-possessed, all dressed up for the night. A new generation of wannabes, all wanting to be there with the Spice Girls reunited under the great dome of the O2.

And me? My pilgrimage is different, less celebration than apology. I have come to make amends for the things I wrote. For the bullying and belittling, for how I appropriated your lives. I'm here to apologise for mistaking my ambitions for yours. For imagining a relationship where there was none. As the poet said, to pray where prayer has been valid.

I am a different person now. I see different possibilities. Shades of grey, not black and white. I can accept that it was always, and only, just music. You became the symbol of a generation when you just wanted to sing and dance and spread a little light. The burden of changing the world was too heavy for such fragile shoulders. And judging by the papers, the glossies, the talk in the classroom these past weeks, it doesn't seem as if the world has changed. The girls in Key Stage 4 still look to the front covers of magazines for a blueprint for life. I generalise, of course, but they aspire to be Kate Moss or Victoria Beckham, not Zadie Smith or Jacqui Smith. Their ambitions seem limited. I admit I'm probably seeing in their relationships with the rich and famous a distorted version of my own back then, but it's sad, all the same. Disappointing.

But, this is not the time. I have moved on. In a matter of minutes, the journey will be at an end. Ten years ago I wanted you to notice me, to pay attention to me. Tonight, when I emerge into the dying light of this December afternoon, I'll be content to be just one of the crowd. You won't even know I'm here and that is as it should be. Now, I am happy to listen to the music and enjoy it. Not fare well, but fare forward. I come now, to applaud. Nothing more, nothing less.

Commissioned as part of the BBC Radio 4 series *From Fact To Fiction* and broadcast on Saturday 15th December, 2007

Half in Love
Amanda Craig

Amanda Craig is the author of five novels, including *A Vicious Circle*, *In a Dark Wood* and *Love in Idleness*. Her sixth, *Hearts & Minds*, will be published next year. She is married, has two children and is children's critic of *The Times*.

There was no denying it: Polly's father was dying at a very inconvenient time. For weeks, she had been organising her family's survival during her absence. Other mothers seemed to manage weekends or even weeks away, blithely going off for holidays in Paris or Prague, conferences in New York or health spas in the countryside, but she had spent thirteen years without a break. Now, she had no choice. A supermarket delivery ordered on the internet would come when things were due to run out. Polly had cooked and frozen several meals which only needed to be reheated, instructed Theo on which route to take when driving the children to school and practised taking them back on the bus.

'You don't have to do this,' said her daughter, crossly. 'I'm not some teeny-weeny ickle cry-baby.'

'You might think that now, but you're only eleven. You might find it a bit more confusing than you think, when you're on your own,' Polly answered.

Her departure had to be organised with military precision. She had chosen flights which coincided with a dip in her work-load, shuffling cases around and toiling at weekends in order to make four days free. She had marked her absence on calendars, and in emails, so that everyone from her colleagues to her cleaner knew when she would be gone. Even so, Theo reacted with horror when it finally dawned on him that she would be gone the following week.

'What? But I'm flying to German on Wednesday for a very important meeting! Can't you cancel it?'

'No, I'm afraid not,' said Polly. 'My father is dying, you see.'

She could see irritation in his face. This was a man who had got her to have a caesarean section when their first child was due to be born in order to fit in with his schedule, and had then taken only half a day of paternity leave. He had an important career as a lawyer in the City; Polly's life, as a part-time solicitor, always had to make way for his, and for the children's needs.

It would have been nice to have had some help from her own mother, but Sarah had made it clear that she was not cut out to be a traditional grandmother. It was their father, Ben, who preoccupied her more. Sarah, too, had combined motherhood with a career, in her case aided by a succession of au pairs; she was impatient with Polly's eternal work-life crisis.

'Lucy has been over to see him four times since the summer,' she told Polly. 'Just come, before he goes.'

'It's not easy to jump on a plane at the drop of a hat, you know.'

'Yes, it is. Just do it, Polly. You won't regret it.'

Polly's parents had retired to the South of France.

'I'm fed up with Britain,' Ben said. 'It's become a nasty, noisy, impatient place. People here still have time to smell the flowers and listen to the birds sing.'

They loved their life in Provence, in the house they had bought when Polly and her sister had been young. It wasn't just the sun, which warmed their increasingly arthritic bones; it was living close to nature. Sarah was a passionate gardener, and Ben a bird-watcher. Sometimes, Ben would ring his daughter just to tell her about the birds he had seen on their hillside: not just ordinary birds, but thrilling buzzards circling over the valley, white barn owls, and the invisible, trilling nightingales that haunted the woods below.

'Listen, darling, can you hear it singing?' he would ask; and faintly, Polly could hear the distant bubbling sound that had almost vanished from her country, and which to her father was the quintessence of the Mediterranean.

But it is one thing to retire to France at sixty-five, and another at nearly eighty; and one thing to live in a holiday home during the summer, and another to live in it during winter. The bitter cold of their Provencal *mas* was barely dented by open fires, the only source of heating because Sarah refused to get central heating.

'I like the smell of a proper fire,' she would say. 'People survived for centuries like this, and besides, it's bad for the furniture. It's like all this nonsense about hygiene; no wonder children have so many allergies.'

Slowly, over the past three years, Polly and Lucy had watched their father dwindle, like a candle burning down. He had been a tall, strong, Vikingly man, but now they were taller than he was. Bent and bald, he became a wheezing voice on the telephone, saying tremulously, 'I do love you so much, my darling. I think about you all the time.'

'I love you too, Pa.'

He never asked her to visit; he knew that, unlike Lucy, she had more commitments, but Polly tried. She would bring the family over in the summer, something they never enjoyed quite as much as she hoped, because Tania and Robbie were selfish, in the way of children, and didn't understand how their high-pitched voices set his hearing-aid ringing. Now, though, she was on a plane, scudding over a miniature landscape sprinkled with snow. London had been blooming in the sunlight of early spring, but here the Mistral was blowing. Icy winds tossed the olives so that their boughs streamed like disorderly silver hair, and the cypress stooped submissively before each blast.

'How is he?' Polly asked, kissing her mother at the airport.

'So-so. He has better days and worse days.'

'Is the cancer still growing?'

'Inevitably. But we muddle on.'

Sarah drove briskly along the winding roads, and always looked so well organised that it was a shock to re-enter the house, and see the usual mess, dirt and dinginess of what had once been a charming holiday home.

'Hasn't Francoise been?' Polly asked.

'Yes, yes, but she always tries to throw things away and get rid of cobwebs,' said her mother. 'She doesn't understand, like most peasants.'

Polly's father was sitting, wrapped in a scarf and overcoat, in the tiny sitting room by the fire. The stink of smoke was overwhelming; he was poking irritably at a log of olive-wood that had fallen out of the grate.

'You silly man, you've only made it worse!' Sarah scolded. She picked up the log with a pair of tongs.

Ben looked terrible. His face was yellowish white, apart from his nose which was a mass of broken red veins; his withered hands were almost blue at the nails. Polly kissed him, and began to chafe his hands gently. The skin was so frail that she was afraid it might tear.

'You should wear gloves, Pa.'

'Hate them. Did you bring my sausages and pork pie?'

'Yes, I did, though why you need them in a country full of lovely charcuterie is a mystery.'

'French food is rubbish. All the Brits living here complain about not being able to get decent sausages. They're all full of garlic.'

'But garlic is good for you,' said Sarah, reprovingly. To Polly, she murmured, 'He just wants the food he ate as a child. He can't eat much, just mush, because of his teeth.' She raised her voice. 'There, I've put another log on the fire again, Ben. Aren't we cosy?'

Polly smiled, but the truth was, they were not cosy at all. Her bedroom was arctic, and her parents' little better. Ben now slept on a bed in the living room, the warmest room in the house, but it was still horrifyingly primitive. Only half the *mas* had been restored; the other half was crumbling into the courtyard like cheese. Overhead, death-watch beetle ticked in the beams, and every time a gust of particularly strong wind blew, the lights flickered and sometimes fused. Her parents had no reading lights, other than the single spotlight which they both squabbled over, and perhaps that was why they failed to see how smeared the windows were, or how thick the dust. Polly always had fantasies about setting the house to rights, like a latter-day Flora Poste, but the reality was beyond her energies. Sarah threw nothing out, and now English newspapers and magazines were piled in towering piles, alongside paperback thrillers, cardboard boxes and plastic bags.

'Don't touch those!' she shrieked, when Polly made a move to burn some of the papers.

How her mother kept things going in these conditions was remarkable. Damp bloomed in continents across the whitewashed walls, now tinted a pale yellowish grey, and her parents' two cats hunted for mice in the woodpile by the fireplace. There was no hot water unless she remembered to turn on the electric boiler a couple of hours before it was needed, and her mother refused to wash up in anything but cold, so all the plates and cutlery were greasy.

'Don't waste the hot water!' she would call, whenever Polly tried to clean. The water whistled and trilled in the pipes – narrowed, like arteries, with calcium.

'I hate living like this,' her father muttered.

'Why don't we go out for lunch?' Polly asked, trying to be cheerful. At least in a café or bistro, her parents would be warm.

'The wind's too cold.'

Once again, a log rolled forward, and filled the room with smoke, setting Ben coughing and wheezing. He had to take regular inhalations of Ventolin. but his thin chest rose and fell with alarming speed. Her mother was constantly trying to get him to eat more tomatoes ('Come on! They help fight those free radicals!' she would say. If Sarah had been able to, she would have bossed around the cells of his body like a Head Girl), but what they really needed was better heating. When Polly opened a window to try and let the smoke out, her father would whimper about the cold.

'Close the door.'

'Get up and close it yourself,' Sarah said.

'I can't,' Ben wheezed, furious.

'If you don't make yourself move, you'll become a permanent invalid.'

It was clear that this was precisely what Ben was, and Polly raged on her father's behalf. She had always been closer to him, while Lucy took her mother's part; but it was also true that Sarah nursed their father with patience. A dozen times a day, she would search out the particular vest he wanted, or help him rise from the toilet. It was like looking after a toddler, although her children's love felt more like being eaten alive. Tania and Robbie didn't like their grandparents, partly because they simply didn't know them but also out of the fear the young feel for the old.

'He's so whiskery,' Robbie whispered to his

mother, 'I don't like kissing him, or her, because of the *bristles*.'

'And their breath smells,' said Tania. 'Why don't they brush their teeth properly?'

'They're just old,' Polly said. 'Be kind to them, they love you and give you nice presents, remember?'

'Yes, but they're so *ugly*,' said Robbie. He was the spitting image of Polly's mother, and sometimes when she cuddled him she had a dizzying foreknowledge of what he would look like as an old man, long after she herself was dead.

Poor boy, she thought; poor boy. So this is how it will be for them, too, one day.

It was strange being here, in winter and without her family. In summer, when they visited, they lived so much out of doors that the acute discomfort of the house mattered less, but now whenever she passed the shrouded swimming pool she was assailed by memories of her children, jumping joyously in. Here, brown as frogs, they had dived or sunned themselves, and in these wild, untended groves she had walked as a teenager herself, enchanted by the mysterious, twisted, dryad-like forms of the olive trees, or swum in the greenish waters of the pool. In winter, these charms were absent. It took an hour to run a bath, the pipes straining, and it was the only time Polly ever got warm. Even wearing thermal socks and vest (which, to her shame, she barely changed because laundry seemed like such an effort) she was freezing. Her father hated it even more than she did. Every so often, when Sarah was out of the room, he would unwrap a packet of firelighters, and defiantly throw a white cube onto the first, where it would flare up for a brief, glorious moment with an evil oily smell and a brilliant flame.

'*Rage, rage against the dying of the light,*' he mumured.

Sarah would always tell him off, furiously.

'You silly old man, you could set yourself on fire if you topple over, don't you see?'

Polly stayed up with him, trying to give Sarah a break.

'Do you remember how you loved to climb that place at the bottom of the waterfall?' her father whispered. Polly smiled lovingly at him.

'Yes, I do. That's where the nightingales sang loudest, wasn't it?'

'I remember how I'd watch you, terrified, and then there was the time when you were almost at the top and a wasp stung your hand, and you let go. You took such risks, then.'

'Yes, I did. I didn't know what I had to lose.'

'Don't be afraid, my darling. A life lived in fear is only half a life.'

Polly stroked his cold hands, their long, knotted

fingers like winter roots.

'I still think of you and Lu as girls, even though I know you're not.'

She laughed, but it was true that she felt more like a girl with her parents than a middle-aged mother. Looking at how wrinkled they were, she felt her own skin to be once again smooth and plump, whereas normally she compared it to her children's unlined perfection, and sorrowed over the erosion of her youth. She massaged her father's shoulders, feeling the curved spine beneath her fingers, frail as that of a dried leaf.

'Are you in pain, darling?'

'Constantly. But *she* doesn't realise. If only she'd let me have some wine.'

All through her life, whenever Ben had seen some elderly person shuffling along with the aid of a zimmer-frame, he had said, 'If ever I get to be like that, just shoot me. Promise me, Polly, you'll shoot me.'

Now, however, he was in a far worse state than those. He could actually walk quite well, for a brief few paces, holding on to supports, and a stick, but Sarah watched him anxiously and, it seemed to her daughter, with barely controlled impatience.

'Be careful, Ben. The last time you fell, it took me twenty minutes to get you back up on your feet. If my back goes, then everything goes.'

'Oh, be quiet, woman. Can't you see I'm in pain?'

'Moan, moan, moan,' said Sarah. 'You shouldn't be in pain, you're on enough pills to kill a horse.'

'Well, a horse doesn't have what I do, does it?'

It was like living with her own children, only worse. For years, Polly's parents had quarrelled, but they had been the quarrels of a tempestuous love affair. They had stuck it out, triumphantly, despite sulks and spats, and if Polly's own marriage was an altogether more placid affair, she and her sister watched as fascinated, half-apprehensive spectators. Now, it seemed, all that was gone.

'He's driving her mad,' Lucy told her before Polly came out. 'Honestly, Pol, she's a saint the way she puts up with his temper. You've got to help her keep his drinking under control.'

'Pa's always drunk more than is good for him, Lu, but Mum drinks too', Polly said.

'Not in the same way.'

Polly had watched her parents put away a litre of wine at lunch and another at dinner when Ben was well – but now Sarah tried to stop her father from having any wine.

'The doctor says it's good for me.'

'Rubbish. If you combine it with your pills, it could kill you. You know drink makes you even more tottery than you are before.'

'I'm not tottery! Tell me one time when I've fallen over because of drinking!'

'On February 12, at that lunch of Liz Sugden's,' said Sarah, crisply.

'That wasn't drink, woman, that was tripping over an uneven floor. Bloodly Provencal floor tiles,' said Ben.

'It was the *drink*,' said Sarah, in exasperation. 'It's dangerous for you.'

'It isn't just the totteriness, he gets so *nasty*,' said her mother, afterwards. 'If he has more than a couple of glasses, you know what he's like, and he just won't stop.'

'I know.'

'It's as if he has a complete personality change,' said her mother. Polly remembered this only too well. When her father was in his cups, his good-natured enthusiasm always vanished. He had ranted at Theo for being what he called 'a stiff-necked American prick', at Polly for being 'such a surrendered mother that you can't even find your own bum,' and at her children for being 'selfish, self-centred little pigs.' All the brave, mad side of him would roar up, like an all-devouring flame.

At the same time, he was so pitiful in his need.

'Just another little drink, Pol. She won't know.'

'But she would, Pa.'

'It's the only thing I have left which gives me any pleasure,' Ben said. 'I can't eat anything except mush, I can't read, I can't listen to music, I can't have sex – '

'Yes, it is terrifically bad luck, Pa,' said Polly hastily. Sex indeed, she thought indignantly: how could he expect it when they were both eighty? Her mother had told her what a relief it was to have separate beds these days. Yet she could see how her father still longed to be touched. The greatest pleasure he had was when one of the two cats jumped on his lap and condescended to lie there, with Ben's cold hands in its thick soft fur.

She doesn't love him any more, she thought sadly. Sarah was still active and energetic; she maintained the half-acre garden far better than she did the house, and liked entertaining and seeing other retired British people in the area, whom Ben had no time for.

'They're all such Philistines,' he said. 'They come here because the booze is cheap, not because of Matisse. Just a little drink, Pol.'

'No, darling.'

'*O for a beaker full of the warm South / With beaded bubbles winking at the brim,*' he said, looking at her with eyes like faded cornflowers.

'My favourite poem,' she said; 'Do the nightingales still sing here?'

'Every year. I'd like to hear them one more time.'

'Oh Pa, you will,' she said, almost crying. 'This beastly wind won't last forever, and soon the spring will be here, and then the summer. Look, the cherry trees are all in blossom, and the primroses are out. It won't be long.'

'The nightingales will sing, but not for me,' he said.

Outside, the sun was shining heatlessly, a clear, relentless light that etched every line on his haggard face. His thoughts were tossed about, like the frantic birds fleeing from tree to tree outside.

'I used to love her so much,' he said; 'but she's become so hard, Pol, so hard.'

'Poor Ma. This must all be a tremendous strain on her.'

'On *her*! She has no idea what a strain it is on *me*. Life just isn't fun any more, Pol. Sometimes I'm in such pain, I cry out, and instead of being sympathetic she glares at me.'

It was true, Sarah did; but then Polly's father was impossible to live with. He would bellow her name, over and over, for the slightest thing, and unable to hear her reply would become ever more furious at being ignored.

'Yes, Ben, it is *coming*,' Sarah would call, with heavy irony. To Polly, she said bitterly, 'He never thanks me, you know.'

Was this what awaited her, and Theo? Polly tried to imagine her husband becoming as weak and frail as her father, in thirty years' time. He, too, was a tall, handsome man but she had married him partly because he was so very different from Ben. Where her father was impetuous, unreasonable, romantic and sentimental, Theo had proposed to her in the manner of a businessman, suggesting a ,convenient arrangement of mutual benefit to both parties. At the time she had taken it as evidence of his delightful sense of irony. Now, however, she realised it was true.

How can I bear it? Polly thought, shivering in her solitary bed at night. She had rung home every day to find out how the children's day had gone.

'Fine. Dad's got everything under control, I don't know why you make such a *fuss*.'

The Mistral howled down the chimney, sending more smoke into the living room.

'What are you doing there, Mum?' her son asked.

'Mostly, putting logs on the fire.'

'That doesn't sound very interesting.'

Sometimes, she wondered what she was doing there, other than acting as a witness to her parents' incessant bickering. After two days, the Mistral suddenly stopped. It rained, and the air became warmer.

'Look, the sun's come out,' said Sarah, putting on her glasses to count out Ben's pills. 'Maybe we could go outside if it stays like this, just for a breath of fresh air.'

'What's the point?' said Ben. 'It's all cold and ugly. Oh, how I hate France!'

Her mother went for a bath, and an afternoon nap; Ben, who slept through much of the morning and afternoon, now woke in the night. Polly could hear the water shrilling in the pipes. She hoped her mother was using the Jo Malone bath oil she had brought her. Sarah looked so, so exhausted.

'Just one more little drink.'

'No, Pa. Maybe later, with supper.'

'No, now. While she's asleep.'

He looked at her with trembling eagerness, and Polly couldn't bear it.

'Just one, mind you.'

She opened a bottle of good Bordeaux, furtively easing out the cork.

'I'll say it was for me.'

'Ah!' he said, sipping. His whole face relaxed, and he smiled. 'Thank you, darling.'

Colour returned to his pale face. Why, all he needed was a little wine, Polly thought, hopefully.

'One more, darling. *A beaker full of the warm South.* You can see it doesn't do me any harm.'

She poured him another. He grinned at her, mischievously, and her heart contracted with love and pain, because he looked himself again.

'That's better.'

He drained it all, determinedly, then gasped for breath.

'Remember: "*for many an hour/I have been half in love with easeful death.*"

'Yes,' Polly said. She understood, now, and stroked his hand tenderly.

'She wouldn't listen,' he said. 'She's been trying to hold on, even when it's just no fun any more.'

'Would you like to try going outside for a moment, dearest Pa? To get out of the smoke and into the light?'

'Yes, darling. You know, I can hear that nightingale singing.'

It was the water in the bath-pipes, but Polly didn't tell him. He smiled, as she buttoned up his coat, wrapped his scarf more securely around his neck, and put his hat on his poor, bald, shrunken head. He stood very erect, like a soldier. Slowly, they walked to the French windows, and stepped out, where the warmth fell on their faces and their eyes dazzled.

'Isn't that beautiful?' said her father.

ChildLine

ChildLine, a service provided by the NSPCC, is the only 24-hour national helpline in the UK that enables children and young people to make a free, confidential call about any issue that is worrying them. ChildLine operates from 11 bases across the UK. With over 1,000 trained volunteers, provides a counselling service supervised by a team of managers with expertise in child protection

Last year, ChildLine answered 175,700 calls from children needing help. However, we can only answer just over half of the calls we receive from children each day. We still have a long way to go before we reach our ultimate aim of answering every call, text or email from every child that needs us.

The NSPCC's vision is to integrate ChildLine with our online counselling service so that every child in the country who needs someone to turn to is offered support on their own terms 24 hours a day, 365 days a year. With your support, we can be there for all children who need our help – no matter why, no matter when.